AUGURY

E.A. Rodriguez

AUGURY

This is a work of fiction. All of the characters, organizations, and events portrayed in this novel is either products of the authors imagination or used fictitiously. Any actual references to person(s) of historical significance are also used fictitiously.

ACKNOWLEDGMENTS

I would like to thank my wife for all her support and pushing me to write this story. Also, I would like to thank Sara Miles-Jewell for helping me edit this book. Gary Bullion, Malinda Garrison and Kayla Dawn, thank you for your input and for putting up with my word vomit.

DESCRIPTIVES

EXT…..EXTERIOR

INT…..INTERIOR

Pronunciations
Belial……….Be-lale
Lailoken……Lyl-lo-cen
Izeta…………Ezata
Dökkálfar…..Doc-al-far
Samhain…….Sow-wen
Tír na nÓg…..Tearn-a-nog

DEDICATION

This book is dedicated to all that I love especially my wife and mother.

BOOK 1

CHAPTER 1
BOOK 1

INT. DIMLY LIT BEDROOM.

The thick dark curtains hang over the large window, concealing the light from the outside. The sky cars of the rich and famous can be heard whizzing past the high rise apartment building. Rayne sits on the edge of the bed leaning over the nightstand, as she writes her break up letter. A few strands of her short, light brown hair dangles free from the hastily wrapped ponytail. She looks back to see that her boyfriend Michael, is in a dead sleep on the other side of the bed. Her brown eyes are glassy with unshed tears. Rayne sets the pen down, then grabs her black, military issue bag, and begins to walk out the room. Rayne takes one last look at Michael before she exits the apartment.

INT. APARTMENT HALL/ELEVATOR

Rayne waits impatiently by the elevator. She doesn't know if she has the strength to confront Michael face to face. They've been through this too many times before and it pains her that this time she has to stick by her word. The intensity of the lights glaring in the hall is like the morning sun, compared to the dim apartment she has just left and stings her eyes. She rubs them to no effect.

She hears the door to Michael's apartment fling open and bang against the wall. Michael strides down the hall in a panic. The thumping of his footsteps beat like a bass drum as he gets closer to turning the corner. He comes into view holding the letter dumbfounded and obviously hurt. His dark shoulder length hair bounces with every determined step. She braces herself to stick with her decision, knowing that it won't only hurt him; it will hurt her as well. Heartbroken, Michael walks up to Rayne.

MICHAEL

"Rayne hold up!"

Michael reaches Rayne. She turns to him wearing her best annoyed look as a mask and a shield. She knows that if she shows him an ounce of regret she's lost.

MICHAEL

Holding the letter in his hand:

"I thought we were working things out. Everything seemed okay. Did I do something wrong?"

RAYNE

"No Mike, you thought that we were going to work things out and everything is not okay. I want something

more than just… this."

She makes a wide panning gesture to include their surroundings.

RAYNE

"I want more than just the four walls of your apartment. I have a chance to live my dream. I have the chance to do something most people can only dream about."

She pauses for a moment, takes a deep breath and readjusts the bag that is slung across her shoulder.

RAYNE

"If I stay here with you it will kill my dream."

Michael quickly interrupts Rayne. Trying to understand her stance on their relationship, he holds his hands up in a placating gesture.

MICHAEL

"Is this about me being kicked out of the military?"

The elevator door opens with a pleasant "ding" sound. Rayne sticks her hand on one of the doors, blocking its sensor to keep the doors open when they try to close.

RAYNE

"No, this is about you openly opposing The North European Union. I have a chance to see the galaxy and if my superiors see that I'm with you, my life, my career is ruined. If I stay I will only end up resenting you for it and it would ruin us and we'd end up hating each other."

Rayne steps into the elevator. For a moment, Michael just stands there stunned at what he has just heard. The doors begin to close, but he snaps out of his stupor and steps in the way. He tries to not let the hurt show on his face, but his eyes give him away. The glassy sheen of moisture glitters as the lights from above reflect in his eyes.

MICHAEL

Holding the elevator doors open. His voice cracks in desperation:

"They took my parents Rayne. They had them executed on unproven crimes. They didn't even get a trial. They got nothing. Nothing! What am I supposed to do?"

Michael never talked much about his family. This was the first time Michael had ever opened up to her about his parents. Aside from a small photo of his mother and father he keeps on his dresser, there is nothing else to suggest that he even speaks to the rest of his family. It hurts Rayne to hear the man she cares about in such pain. She wants to go to him and comfort the man with the single tear rolling down his cheek, but doesn't know what to say. So, for a long moment she says nothing. Her head hanging low so he can't see the tears welling up in her eyes.

RAYNE

"I'm sorry Michael."

Michael's hands fall to his side in defeat as his shoulders slump and his jaw goes slack. He watches the doors to the elevator close. He just stands in the hall staring at the muddled image of himself in the reflective metal doors. His mind is in a daze and his chest numb.

CHAPTER 2

INT. T.V. SCREEN

The channels on the holo display flash wildly as they are being surfed. A soft flicking sound can be heard as the receiver switches frequencies and displays a new channel. The viewer skips through countless channels of reality, cooking and game shows then finally stops on a news station.

The headlines read: Dec. 22, 2113 HISTORIC DAY! The news camera is focused on the mobile lattice-like triangular structure that rests in the center of the state of the art Royal air force base. Pilots stand next to their jets in parade rest waiting for the ceremony to begin and their first chance to travel through interstellar space. Crowds of people gather to see the achievement of their top scientists in eager anticipation and pure wonderment. For them it's like watching man take his first steps on the moon. A smaller group of people surrounded by security can be seen off to the side protesting the device they see as an abomination.

A young and stunning African American woman stands to the right of the viewable portion of the holographic projection. A

wide shot of the RAF (Royal Air Force) Barkston Heath Base,
fills the background with the triangular structure at its center.

FEMALE REPORTER

"A historic announcement has been made by Chancellor
Belial. The Hyper Jump Gate Program that has been in
development for decades, may be yielding its fruits on
this very evening. He has told sources that the project is
ready for use and the commencement ceremony is set to
begin in a matter of moments."

INT. MICHAEL'S LIVING ROOM

The voices from the news broadcast begin to fade as Michael,
along with a few close friends, sit on couches around his
gathering room partaking in idle chat and alcoholic beverages.
The dimly lit room is a typical room for a man, the drapes hang
off of the window partially exposing the gleaming metal and
glass metropolis. Bright lights of speeding crafts zip by outside.

Tamari, a slender woman of about twenty four years of age
wears her dark hair in two short spiky pigtails on either side of
her head, which is one of the latest fashions. Her small black
vest is unbuttoned and her white blouse hangs loosely off her
body. She knows why they are all here and she is always there
for her friends when they need her. She has known Michael
since middle school and thinks of him as a brother. She knows
he needs to keep his mind off of the events of the day before.
Michael lurches off the couch and heads into the kitchen.

TAMARI

"So, you're saying that you stole a prototype from your dad and it does what exactly?"

The lanky Englishman pushes his big soda bottle glasses further up on the bridge of his nose before he takes hold of the device in question. Holding the T.D.B.(Temporal Drift Band) in hand. Leaf tries to put what he knows of the thing into words. The armband is a sleek metallic gauntlet that wraps around the forearm of the user with three small display screens.

LEAF

"My dad calls it a Temporal Drift Band. It's supposed to let you go through time or something, to observe and learn or some shit."

KAT

"Why to observe the past? Wouldn't it be better to go through and tear some shit up and mess with people? Or you could go back fact check the Bible, or even the history books and put an end to all these fanatics roaming the streets."

Kat rolls the sleeves of her striped shirt higher on her forearms then adjusts the little vintage neck tie that has come to be a trade mark of sorts for her. Joe takes a puff of his stim stick, exhales and addresses Kat who is now busy untying her black boots.

JOE

"You can't."

"Haven't you ever heard of the Grandfather Paradox? Knowing you, you'd sleep with some guy and become your own great grandmother or something crazy like that."

KAT

"Who cares about your grandfather?"

They all laugh. Kat leans down to set her boots off to the side of the small coffee table and wiggles her toes as she stretches and combs her fingers through her short blue hair.

TAMARI

Still chuckling at Kats remark:

"You can't be serious. The Grandfather Paradox is when you go back in time, do something that alters the future. You may even kill your own grandfather and then you would have never been born. Then there is no way you could have traveled back to begin with and it causes the universe to implode or something."

Kat stretches out on the couch, waiting for Michael to come back into the room. She looks in Tamari's direction and answers in a completely serious tone.

KAT

"I know what it is. I was just saying who cares about his grandfather."

Weary and a bit incredulous of the strange direction the conversation had gone so fast, Leaf continues with his explanation.

LEAF

"Well, anyway, that paradox is why it's still a prototype. The government doesn't want it getting out and into the wrong hands."

INT. KITCHEN

Michael has just finished reading the letter left by his now ex girlfriend for what seemed like the thousandth time, then tosses it into the waste bin. He heads into the living room to join the conversation. He doesn't realize it but Kat can't help but look at him with hungry eyes. She stretches again making sure to really arch her back accentuating her breasts. She has had a crush on Michael for years and was always jealous of Rayne. With her female competition seemingly out of the picture, she was going to make her move.

Michael snatches the T.D.B. out of Leaf's hands as he walks out of the kitchen and sits on the floor in front of the couch. He brushes the few strands of hair that was not caught by his ponytail out of face.

MICHAEL

"If they didn't want it getting into the wrong hands they really shouldn't have given the thing to your dad and tightened up security. I bet that if they knew that he had a son who is an underground activist, they would have had him black bagged and beaten with wiffle ball bats for hours on end."

Michael looks at the T.D.B. and plays with the tiny switches before putting it on his wrist. It seems familiar to him but he chucks it up to the thing looking fancy.

KAT

"Beaten with wiffle ball bats? I'm pretty sure they have other things that they could be doing to make our lives just a tad more miserable. Like death from a thousand paper cuts. Like they do to those nut jobs who think they're warlocks or mages of old."

Kat's comment hurt Michael. He had never told them how his parents were accused of being members of such a secret society. In fact, the same group of "Nut jobs" who had come out of hiding five years ago in the hopes of being able to better protect themselves from being "Black Bagged" was the very same order his parents had once belonged. He didn't know all the facts about that group, yet he felt sorry for them. Hell, he didn't find out his parents belonged to such a group until a few months ago when his uncle Taven had finally told him. He had always wondered why he had a forged identification card and birth records but the big picture was still obscure and still too big for

him to see at the moment. To cover his brief moment of
depression, Michael quickly paints a mask of one who thinks
the mindset of those "Nut Jobs" was esoteric and completely
crazy.

MICHAEL CONT'D

"I don't think those people know what they are talking
about. I mean who in their right mind would actually
admit to being a part of an ancient secret society of
witches? It's utter bullshit. But before I lose my train of
thought-Why would the universe implode if you were to
kill your grandfather? Wouldn't you just create an
alternate timeline where you wouldn't exist? Like a fork
in the road?"

Leaning over in his seat Joe smacks Leaf in the arm jokingly
and makes an obscene gesture with his hands and mouth.

JOE

"I think that's why your dad tries so hard to please the
top brass."

Leaf shakes his head at the shamelessness of the people whom he
chooses to associate with.

LEAF

"Either way, it's a secret project. I knew I shouldn't have
shown you shit. All you ever do is bust my balls and tell
me how much of a tool my father is. Yes Michael, it could
cause the timeline or universe to splinter, at least in

theory."

Kat leans in closer to Michael to get a better look at the sleek device. She leans in even closer when he does not notice her, so she readjusts herself so that she can be as near to her secret crush without being too obvious and letting the others know her intentions, though they already knew why she chose to hang out tonight.

MICHAEL

"I knew that shit they taught in school about time travel being impossible was bullshit. Twenty years ago they were saying that traveling to other star systems in a short time was never gonna happen because we couldn't break the light speed barrier, and look, tonight they're gonna do it."

Kat raises her eyebrows and scoots toward Michael so that their faces are inches apart.

KAT

"So are ya' gonna do it?"

MICHAEL

"Do what? Go through time? Uh no. I couldn't live without my "Novas"."

TAMARI

"You can't stand to part with your Nova? Really? Not your aunts or girlfriend, fuck your friends. A video game? Just like a man, always trying to escape reality."

Kat nods and supports Tamari. She could think of a few things he'd miss if only she could pry his attention in her direction and arrange for some alone time.

JOE

"Now ladies, leave the poor man alone. You'd be salty too if your girlfriend dumped you every other day and your parents had died in a horrible traffic accident when you were young, causing you to be bounced around with different family members like a nomad."

MICHAEL

Squinting at Joe with mock displeasure:

"I'm not sure if that's supposed to make me feel better. Thanks I think?"

All but Kat laugh again. Joe, fidgets in his seat, working up the nerve to address the reason why they've come to cheer their friend up. With all mockery aside, Joe asks the question that has been on the mind of almost everyone present.

JOE

"So why did, Rayne leave you this time?"

Michael takes a moment to gather his thoughts. He would rather have them completely ignore the drama in that part of his life and continue on as they have been, but he knows that's not what he needs at this moment. He toys with the notion of completely blowing off the question or lying to them. He pauses for a few moments as he gathers his thoughts. He tells them just enough to ease their curiosity and vent his mind. He sighs before he answers.

MICHAEL

"She was given a spot on the gate program. The government wouldn't like it if they knew that she was with someone who was dishonorably discharged from the military and turned activist."

Realizing the subject needs to be changed and not just for his sake. Kat speaks up.

KAT

"C'mon Spidy-Mike, you should really go back and kick the shit out of some ancients. You said it yourself, it would only make a fork in the road."

MICHAEL

Points at Leaf:

"Only if it's O.K. with the daddy's boy over there."

The others look at Leaf with pleading expressions and begging gestures while he shakes his head in defiance. After a moment his resolve crumbles and he smiles.

LEAF

"I hate you twats, you know that? Come here I'll show you how to use it."

The three friends celebrate their victory and gather on the couches in the room anticipating the event to come. Feeling underdressed for the occasion, Michael heads into an adjacent room to get suited up.

INT. MICHAEL'S BEDROOM

Michael searches the rubble of clothes and luggage in his closet until he finds his old duffle bag buried under mounds of outfits. Inside the bag he finds his body glove, that he had received when he signed up for the military, the black market body armor and equipment he purchased after being discharged, and two special items he hadn't touched in years. The Equalizer rail gun and an old Accelerated Xiphoid Laser (A.X.L.). Clad in armor and black paramilitary clothes, Michael looks into the mirror hanging on the wall, then at the picture of his parents pasted in its corner. He tucks the picture in his jacket pocket.

INT. ROOM

When Michael enters the room he finds his friends plotting the path he should take through time and talking about what Michael should do when he gets to the past. Most of their ideas are silly and not even worth the time nor the effort.

JOE

"What are you gonna take with you? I mean, you know the ancients are fucking numb-skulls and you may have to put a few of them down."

"Dude you should totally take your fathers Equalizer that thing is vicious."

Michael pulls out the large handgun from its holster attached to his back and checks to see if the accelerators are still functional. He then loads a fresh bar of metal into the intake chamber. The large black gun that is The Equalizer is a gun that shaves off thin sheets of metal from the intake chamber and uses powerful magnets and electrical pulses to propel the shavings at a desired target with such speed and force that the results end in not only penetration but shredding of tissues. It had been outlawed several years ago. Most of the models have been recalled and destroyed. Michael couldn't bring himself to part with his father's weapon.

Michael looks down to see Kat staring at his crotch. Her eyes are glazed and her face is flush with tiny beads of sweat. She looks up to see Michael looking at her curiously and then she realizes that she had been caught. Her cheeks flare in embarrassment as she turns several shades of red in the micro second it takes her to recover and attempt to nullify any suspicions he might have. She points to another object strapped on Michael's upper thigh.

KAT

"He's already ahead of you on that one, but what's that on your hip?"

MICHAEL

"That's my A.X.L."

The A.X.L. is a high powered burning laser device, that extends reflectors that spin at high velocities to make the many lasers seem like a solid bar of light. This tool was favored among construction workers and loggers in the past. It too has long since been deemed a dangerous tool and recalled to the manufacturers for dismantlement. Michael's mother was an emergency responder and she had used this tool to help trapped victims who had been pinned in auto accidents or stuck in collapsed buildings.

JOE

"Wait. You're bringing a construction tool with you? Do you plan on chopping down some trees?"

MICHAEL

"Maybe I am. This thing gets so hot it can cut through solid steel and anything else for that matter. I may need to make my own exit door or something."

KAT

"That thing is so small and like thirty years old and it still works? Damn."

Tamari wraps her arm around Joe's neck as she leans forward off of the couch and on to his back startling him.

TAMARI

"It's not the size of the tool. It's the man using it. Isn't that right honey?"

JOE

"I guess."

Leaf looks over at the couple with a humored expression and turns back to Michael to explain how the device works to the best of his knowledge.

LEAF

"Well that was little too much information."

LEAF CONT'D

Pointing at the displays:

"All right, this will show your position in time and space and keep you from transporting into a tree, rock, or what have you. This is your temporal selector. I set it to send you back here when you're done doing whatever it is you decide to do."

MICHAEL

"What do I do if I want to go to a specific place and time?"

LEAF

"Okay, it's been set to use our dating and time keeping

system so punch in the numbers here and boom."

Nervously, Leaf looks around at everyone in the room then back at Michael and whispers.

LEAF CONT'D

"Aye mate, if you don't want to do this you don't have to. Not to please us."

MICHAEL

"Dude, it's cool. What's the worst that can happen? How do I activate it?"

Leaf peers up at Michael through his bespectacled eyes. The look in his eyes speaks volumes of the unknown dangers this device can cause yet, a part of him wants to know the capabilities of time travel. Another huge part screams to stop everything and tell his friend not to go through with this reckless stunt. He ignores his fear and points to the power switch.

JOE

Claps his hands together ready for the show:

"Alright everybody get back! It's Show time!"

As Michael turns on the T.D.B. the others are silent, watching intently as the impossible is about to take place right before their eyes. The news broadcast fills the room with the lilting voice of the female reporter.

The small group of friends silently wait for the once in a

*lifetime experience. The news feed from the holo-cast plays on
in the background, as another historic, televised event unfolds
elsewhere. A Detailed view of the Hyper Gate's steel frame fills
the viewing area. The mesh like support beams glint with the
flashing lights of the reporters and the growing crowed. Men
and women in white coats over blue jumpsuits scurry about
attaching power cables and reading diagnostic information on
handheld glass computers.*

FEMALE REPORTER

"Viewers what you are looking at now is the Gate itself.
The engineers are putting on the finishing touches."

*Michael takes two steps back putting some distance between
him and the others in the room. He punches in a series of
numbers that form a date and time into the device then fingers
the ignition. A hum that starts as a whisper and grows in
intensity vibrates through the air of the quiet room. Michael is
surrounded by a transparent blue orb. The eyes of the others
grow wide with disbelief and right before the humming reaches
its climax the machine abruptly shuts down.*

JOE

Arms flinging in the air in disappointment:

"Aw what the fuck!"

*Kat lets loose a sigh of relief as she and Tamari lean back into
the heavily cushioned couch. They exchange a worried look
then turn back to Leaf and Michael. Leaf gets up and heads
over to Michael to check the device to find out why it*

malfunctioned. *The others throw snack foods at him. He flinches as the little edible projectiles strike him.*

LEAF

"Oh. Ah ha! Well, we didn't let it charge up enough before you tried to leave."

TAMARI

"You mean the damn thing takes batteries?"

Michael looks at Leaf, eyes wide with concern that he had left out what would seem to be very important information pertaining to the operations of the device wrapped around his arm.

MICHAEL

"Um that would have been information that I needed know. I don't want to leave and be stuck somewhere looking for a pack of copper tops."

LEAF

"It doesn't take fuckin' batteries! It's self sustaining. The power cells just need to be charged up before being used. What the fuck do you think this is? The 21st century? Fuckin' batteries."

MICHAEL

"How do I set the charge then?"

Leaf shows Michael how to initiate the charge.

LEAF

"You just press here and here."

Leaf pulls up the diagnostic readings of the device and finds the problem. He begins to slowly punch in a series of commands making sure that Michael is watching what he is doing. With a nod of conformation, Leaf steps back.

KAT

"Well, how long does it take?"

JOE

"Don't tell me we have to wait until tomorrow to see this thing work."

LEAF

"No. It'll take maybe five minutes for a full charge... I think."

The digital meter on the tiny display is moving along faster than expected. Michael turns to storm out of the gathering room in a panic due to an afterthought, then turns back to his friends. The others look on in confusion when he whips around to address them.

MICHAEL

"Oh! I have one more thing I have to get before this thing is done."

LEAF

"Really, what else could you possibly need?"

Michael runs into his room and yanks the duffle bag from the closet with such force that the worn strap tears away from the bag causing some items to be tossed onto the floor.

The news broadcast once again fills the silence as Michael rummages through his things in the other room. The Chancellor can be seen walking over to the gate.

FEMALE REPORTER

"In a matter of moments now, Chancellor Belial will flip the switch to activate the Gate."

Finding the item he had been searching for, Michael comes back out strapping a device to his other wrist.

KAT

"Belial's arm is fucking creepy. Does anybody know why his arm is all cybernetic?"

JOE

"Who knows why any of those politicians do what they do. He probably got it mangled when he was kid or something. I mean look at him. He looks like he was in some war."

Michael looks at the screen. The disgust he feels for the man runs deep. He's never met Chancellor Belial, but the vibe he gets at the mere mention of his name is enough to send shivers down his spine.

MICHAEL

"He probably pissed off the wrong person and got it hacked off. He looks like the type of person who would tongue punch your mother in the stink-hole and not even bother to offer her the courtesy of a reach around."

LEAF

Laughing a bit:

"You're not right, mate."

TAMARI

"You're probably right about that though. He looks like the type that's like, lick my nasty creepy cybernetic arm and like it."

They all laugh then the T.D.B. beeps as it finishes charging. The chime grabs the attention of the young group and they all turn to Michael.

LEAF

"Right then. Everybody get back. You sure are a nutter to do something like this mate. Just make sure your ass stays out of trouble."

MICHAEL

"I know, but you guys wouldn't have it any other way."

The loud hum fills the silence, as Michael is once again surrounded by the blue glow. The others watch unblinking as the hum grows loud enough to be felt in their bones. Michael stands blocking the view of the holo cast.

FEMALE REPORTER

"The world watches as this historic moment is finally underway. Less than five minutes remain for the start of a new era in human history that will change our lives forever."

The hum grows to a high pitched whine as it generates the power necessary to rip through the fabric of space and in a flash Michael disappears.

CHAPTER 3

INT. DARK APARTMENT

Michael finds himself in his childhood home. Relief flutters through him as he realizes that the device actually worked. He tenuously walks over to the shelves that hold the family photos. Picking up the exact same copy of the photo he carries in his breast pocket. His eyes water as grief and relief overwhelm his emotions. Taking a moment to compose himself, he takes some time to look around and rediscover old memories.

Michael finds an old toy of his next to an end table in the corner of the room. The stuffed bear from his childhood opens the floodgates to memories, that up until this point, he had forgotten. There is nothing particularly special about the plush toy, but it had meant the world to him. His revelries are cut short when he hears the voices of his parents just outside the front door. Panic hits him when he realizes what his parents might think when they find a well armed man clad in black, standing in the middle of the family room. Frantic, he leaps into the coat closet and pulls the door inches from the latch just as the front door swings open and his parents walk through.

Juanita is the first through the door. She rapidly begins stripping off her thick brown coat. Close behind is Michael's father, John clad in his police uniform and protective body armor. They both seem frightened which sends Michael's stomach twisting into knots. John shuts the door quickly and locks the bolt.

JUANITA

"Do you think we've lost them, John?"

Panic stricken, she begins to pull her loose curly hair into a knot behind her head.

JOHN

"I don't know, but we need to send a message to my brother and let him know he'll have to keep, Michael a little longer than we planned."

Juanita heads to the holo net to send the message.

JUANITA

"I'll send it now."

Michael watches through the slats in the door as his parents scramble to make the call and check the windows for suspicious activity. Emotions flood his already racing mind. Speaking to Michael's uncle in almost inaudible words, Juanita can't help but cry.

JUANITA

"It's not looking too good, Taven. They've found us. I don't know how, but they found us. Please don't tell Michael."

The voice on the other end of the conversation is low and Michael can't make out what is being said on the other end. Juanita begins to sob and her husband moves closer to comfort her. He rubs his hand up and down her back over her thick woven eggshell white sweater.

JOHN

Holding his wife:

"Maybe we're reading too much into this. We don't know if that was him."

JUANITA

Weeping:

"Don't kid yourself John. We knew this day was coming. He's got some vendetta against anyone who shows even the smallest amount of talent."

John knew immediately what "talent" meant. His wife's family had always been considered mystics of sorts. They practice what they call "The Arts" and drew on their "Talent" to add power to their spells or rituals. He had never felt anything but complete admiration for them. He even thought the family members that considered themselves travelers or gypsies were the more fascinating of the bunch. Recently however, family members have either been disappearing or dying of mysterious circumstances. The family had thought it was just bad juju until a second cousin survived long enough to give the rest a heads up and let them know that they were being hunted. Ever since then their joyful life had been nothing except pins and needles.

JOHN

"I know."

Loud heavy footsteps can be heard out in the main hall. Without warning the main door shatters into splinters, then men in black paramilitary fatigues pour through the opening followed by a man, Michael can't see.

John steps in front of his wife to protect her. One of the men in full riot gear quickly stretches out his arm, then violently pulls John down to the floor and restrains him. The man leading the band of soldiers saunters around the room examining family photos and trinkets. He knocks over crystal family heirlooms until he comes to a single picture of Michael. The man in charge roughly snatches up the picture frame, snapping it as he rips the photo out of its protective casing. With the speed of a viper he shoves the photo in Juanita's face.

Anxiously Michael stands in the closet desperately and silently trying to find a better position so he can see the man interrogating his mother. Face down on the floor with a knee in his back, John struggles to get free.

SHADOW MAN

"Where is he?"

JOHN

"What do you want? We don't even know you!"

A pistol is pressed against the back of John's head. At the sight of the firearm, Juanita shrieks in terror, for she knows that this may be their last moments on Earth. She didn't even get a chance to say good bye to her son. Juanita continues to sob as the armed men restrain the both of them. The pressure on John's neck feels like his bones would pop free of his skull. John knew that if the bear of a man that was on top of him would put just an ounce more weight on him that his neck would snap. Juanita can hear and feel the industrial strength zip ties being locked into place. The tough plastic bands bite into her skin at the wrists and elbows.

SHADOW MAN

"Oh, but I know you and what you represent. This is the last time I am going to ask. Where is the boy?"

Indecision and fear hold Michael in a tight grip. He knows that if he intervenes now there is a good chance he will be killed, but on the other hand, if he acts his parents may live. The choices eat at the very core of his soul as he inwardly argues with himself.

Juanita's sniffles grow quiet and less frequent as she gathers her resolve. She's come to terms with her fate. She glares at each one of the men she can see, before finally stopping and meeting the eyes of the man calling the shots.

JUANITA

Anger filling her voice:

"Leave us alone you sick..."

Her words are cut short by the powerful hand that shot out to clench her throat. Juanita struggles and fights for air, but the men holding her arms behind her back won't allow her to budge. John struggles in vain to get free and help his wife. The man holding John smashes the butt of the gun against the back of the restrained man's head. Increasing his grip around the helpless woman's neck, the shadowy man leans in close so that he can look her in the eyes.

SHADOW MAN

"Listen to me you mutt bitch. I am going to spend many months eeking out every ounce of suffering from your soul. By the time I am done, you will crave for an end to your misery. First, I am going to break you. I am going to destroy you so completely that you will be a tired husk when I am done. I will ensure that you suffer many indignities before I finally put an end to you and I will still kill your son. Let your mind wonder on that for a while."

The iron grip around Juanita's throat is released and she crumples to the floor gasping for air. The armed men holding her grab a hand full of hair and yank her head back up.

The Shadowy man makes a gesture and the armed men holding Michael's mother begin to drag her out of the apartment. A bird squawks outside the window. One of the men holding John produces another side arm and both men almost simultaneously shoot his father in the head.

The sound of the gunshot triggers something within. Michael leaps out of the closet toward the shadowy man and see's that the man threatening his parents, is Chancellor Belial. The shock of it gave Michael pause for only a second but that second was enough for Belial to smile, lift his fist in the fastest back hand Michael had ever seen and send the dismayed man crashing through the window of the high rise apartment building.

There is nothing but the shock and gut wrenching feeling of failure as Michael plummets to the streets below, passing inches from air traffic, that if they collided he would surely be killed. He can remember looking out that very window and thinking, "My, how they all look like ants from up here" but with the view of the ground rapidly approaching, Michael finally snaps back to his senses and begins to frantically push buttons on the display and just as he is about to crash on some gesticulating fat woman he disappears.

CHAPTER 4

EXT. GRAVEL ROAD - GERMANY

On a road surrounded by trees and thick brush, the birds sing carefree as they fly over head. It's the middle of the day and two German soldiers are enjoying their booze and are about to light another cigarette.

GERMAN SOLDIER SCHMIDT

Takes a drink from the bottle of alcohol then passes the half empty bottle back to the other soldier:

"Wo haben Sie diese bekommen? Es brennt. "

(Where did you get this? It tastes like acid.)

GERMAN SOLDIER WEBER

Takes a drink:

"Verstanden weg von einem toten Amerikaner."
(Got it off of a dead American.)

Takes another drink:

"Ich werde in kürzester Zeit getrunken werden."

(I'll be drunk in no time.)

The men light their cigarettes to help quell the burn in their throats. The soldiers carry important Intel on Russian troop movements, that they should have reported to their superiors, but neither of the men ever wanted any part in this war to begin with. They only wanted to spare their families from imprisonment and possible execution.

GERMAN SOLDIER SCHMIDT

"Wir sollten diese Informationen an den Führer zu bekommen, so dass wir die Russen zu vernichten. "

(We should get this information to the leader so we will crush the Russians.)

GERMAN SOLDIER WEBER

Taking another drink of the booze:

"Der Führer hat sich wirklich mal alles auseinander fallen."

(The leader has really let it all fall apart.)

Flashes of light followed by thunderous booms ripple through the air as Michael falls out of the wormhole and hits the ground just outside of Berlin. The T.D.B. reads: Berlin, 1945, 29 April. As Michael struggles to get his bearings and pick himself up off the ground, he notices a couple of German soldiers glaring at him with eyes as wide as their gaping mouths. Frozen in wonder or absolute shock to see a man appear out of thin air the soldiers just stand there. One of the soldier's cigarette falls from his mouth. The red hot cherry brushes the top of his hand and the man doesn't even flinch. The two men stay this way, for what may have been forty five seconds before Michael stands up. The tendrils of cobalt blue smoke rise off of his body from the drift through time and travels with the gentle breeze. Finally after another thirty seconds the two soldiers react.

GERMAN SOLDIER SCHMIDT

Shaking in fear and pointing a gun at Michael:

"Stopp! Nicht bewegen!"

(Stop! Don't move!)

Michael puts his hands up. The other soldier looks at his bottle of booze, throws it away and proceeds to help his partner. Drawing his gun the soldier approaches Michael slowly and begins shouting.

GERMAN SOLDIER WEBER

"Auf die Knie! Auf die Knie!"

(On your knees! On your knees!)

Michael positions his arms in front of him, pointing his hands at the soldiers and activates a stunningly bright magnesium flash that not only stuns the two men as it burns their retina, but causes them to drop their weapons. The soldiers grab their eyes and fall to their knees screaming.

GERMAN SOLDIERS

"Ich kann nicht sehen!"

(I can't see!)

Michael runs away.

EXT. THE STREETS OF BERLIN

Michael makes his getaway into the ruined streets of Berlin and finds himself standing out among the crowd. Pedestrians cast a suspicious eye as he rushes down the street. Others cross the road or hide inside bombed out shops as he approaches them. He realizes that he has been noticed by a squad of heavily armed men and he quickly ducks into an alley way to escape them and get his mind to stop racing.

EXT. ALLEY

The soldiers never found the strange man who was running down the street and scaring the few citizens left in the city, so they head off to more important matters. The sun has sunk so low in the sky that the alley, like much of the city is dark and empty. The people scramble through the streets looking for a safe place for their families.

Under a mountain of trash that has been piled high against a small business, Michael begins to move. He crawls out from under the foul smelling heap causing parts of the rubble laced debris to roll to the pavement. Michael looks at the T.D.B. and realizes that it had taken him to the wrong time. He tries to reset the device to take him back to his apartment but it shuts down. Its power cell is depleted and requires a recharge. In frustration and anger Michael kicks a metal trash can then leans against what's left of a wall and grunts.

MICHAEL

"What the hell am I gonna do?"

EXT. BERLIN-NIGHTFALL

The shattered city lay in ruins. Distant gun shots travel on the air of the night. Explosions can be heard in the distance but they are definitely getting closer. Planes can be heard in the sky overhead. A couple of streets over, tank treads grind against the hard paved street as patrols and watchmen move about.

EXT. ALLEY- NIGHTFALL

Michael pokes his head out to see if the coast is clear. He exits the alley and walks down the street where he notices a clothing shop that is still standing intact.

Michael looks around, puts on his hood, and breaks the glass of the front window. The glass clatters to the ground so loud that any other time someone would have noticed, but with the war going on he doesn't worry about being caught by the authorities. He makes his way through the small store passing rack upon rack of fancy tailored suits and dresses until he comes to a section that contains nothing but coats. He flicks through the many hangers until he comes to a long black coat with real silver buttons. He grabs the black trench coat and puts it on.

When Michael exits the shop, he can hear more planes in the skies overhead and begins to walk hastily following a mini map on the now slow to charge T.D.B. Making his way toward a hidden bunker that should offer some safety from the clash of arms getting closer to his position, Michael notices a patrol headed his way. He ducks behind some barrels to avoid being spotted. He notices a piece of metal under some grass. He moves the grass aside to reveal a door built into the dirt.

Michael waits until the patrol has passed and the coast is clear, before he pulls on the door. It's locked. Sirens suddenly sound and lots of dogs bark into the night. Search lights hit the sky illuminating the dark clouds to reveal planes high above and they seem to be disintegrating before his eyes. Then he realizes that the planes are not coming apart, they're dropping bombs.

Soldiers fill the streets scrambling to get to their positions. In the grip of panic, Michael crouches low and tries to get an idea of what's going on around him. He pulls out his father's gun. Anti aircraft guns begin to fire into the sky. Bombs begin to hit the buildings near Michael. The concussive force of so many explosions going off at once near him jars his body and throws him to the ground. Ears ringing, Michael shoots off the lock to the door, opens it and jumps in. He grabs hold of the metal ladder and begins to climb down.

INT. TINY SHAFT

A bomb explodes above, near Michael's last position with such force that it shreds the thick steel entry port, mangling the top half of the ladder and sending a shock wave down the steel rungs knocking him off the ladder. Michael drops the rest of the way down and crashes to the hard concrete floor.

INT. BUNKER

The dim lights flicker with each thunderous boom from above. Shaking the stars from his vision, Michael gets to a crouched position. Soldiers can be heard in the other wings of the bunker shouting commands at their subordinates.

Making his was down the narrow corridor, Michael thinks that he has avoided detection and just might get out of this alive. He thinks this, right until he feels the barrel of a gun touch the back of his head. Michael stops. He raises his hands tentatively, then in a flash, he turns around grabbing the gun and striking the soldier in the throat. The soldier falls to the floor choking. The man pulls out a knife worthy of Rambo's praise and before the man can get to his feet, Michael shoots him. The shot bounces off the narrow walls sending sharp daggers in the form of sound waves to assault his ears. Michael drops the gun in shock at what he had just done. He slowly steps away from the dead Nazi, turns and begins to run.

He comes to an intersection in the hallway and spots two guards standing in front of a big metal door. Slow unsteady footsteps echo down another hall heading for the guards.

Michael peeks out from the wall and sees a man talking to the guards. They salute him and leave. The man limps up to the door, opens it and walks inside. His gait seems so strange and labored. The man left the door ajar. Looking down at the time band, Michael can see that it is now charged, but his niggling curiosity gets the better of him. Michael notices that there is an odd silence in the bunker and creeps up to the large door to have a look inside. Michael can't see anything. He steps inside the door and into a poorly light room.

INT. BUNKER

Michael can hear two men and a woman talking. One seems to be calm yet aggravated, and the other seems to be in a state of panic. The woman in the room weeps uncontrollably. He stays in the shadows and makes his way closer to see them, making sure not to make a sound.

MAN

"Was denken Sie, Sie tun? "

(What do you think you are doing?)

HITLER

Hands held together as if in prayer:

"Mein Herr, ich weiß nicht, wie alles schief ging. "

(My lord, I don't know how it all went wrong.)

EVA

Begging and sobbing:

"Bitte mein Herr, erbarme. Ich will nicht sterben. "

(Please my Lord, show mercy. I don't want to die.)

MAN

"Sie scheitern an unsere Ordnung in die Welt zu bringen und Sie um Gnade bitten? "

(You fail to bring our order to the world and you ask for mercy?)

Michael tries to get a look at the man but cannot see his face. He cannot risk getting any closer. The massive stone column he is using as cover is the last one he can safely stand behind without being noticed by the occupants in the room.

HITLER

"Mein Herr ... "

(My Lord)

The man throws Eva a vile of clear liquid. She barely catches it with both hands. She looks at the small corked glass and the liquid inside. Realization crashes over her face. She looks back at the man with a pleading expression in her eyes that does little to hide the fear in her heart.

MAN

"Nehmen Sie es. "

(Take it.)

Eva opens the vile and looks up to Adolf, worried. She frantically searches his eyes for some kind of support, but only finds a grim resignation. Her shoulders slump, the tears freeze in her eyes and she begins to quiver uncontrollably.

The man in the grey coat produces a Luger pistol and points it at the head of Eva. She yelps in surprise and grips the small vile with her other hand to steady it, trying not to shake it or spill its contents. The tears begin to flow from her eyes once again while she tries to steel her nerves.

MAN

"Nehmen Sie es, oder ich werde dir ins Gesicht zu schießen! "

(Take it or I'll shoot you in the face!)

HITLER

"Mein Herr, bitte. "

(My Lord, please.)

MAN

"Sie haben bis drei zählen. Eins, zwei ... "

(You have until the count of three. One, two...)

Eva lifts the vile to her lips, jerks her head back, and swallows the poison in one swig. Moments later she starts to gag as a foamy substance fills and boils out of her mouth. She looks back at Adolf, with a look that screams of shattered trust. Her body spasms in rapid uncontrollable movements. She quickly dies. Satisfied, the man points his gun at Adolf and calmly waits.

HITLER

Hands held out:

"Ich werde nicht wieder scheitern Sie, Herr. "

(I will not fail you again, my Lord.)

MAN

"Das wird nie wieder passieren. "

(This will never happen again.)

HITLER

Eyes closed:

"Ich schwöre, das wird nie wieder passieren. "

(I swear this will never happen again.)

The man shoots Hitler in the head. The impact of the 9mm bullet rocks the small man back in his chair spraying chunks of skull and brain matter out the other end and onto the hard concrete floor. His head violently rocks back then his body slumps forward and his head lolls from side to side before coming to stop. The man places the gun in Hitler's hand, then

*turns and leaves the room out of a separate exit. Michael can't
believe what he just saw.*

*When the man's footsteps are far enough away Michael leans
on the pillar. A torrent of unanswered questions fills his head
and he almost feels sorry for the doomed lovers. He cautiously
steps out from behind the stone pillar and creeps up to the
deceased.*

MICHAEL

In shock at what he's just witnessed:

"What the hell just happened?"

*Michael turns on the T.D.B. and rapidly punches in the date to
his own year making sure to include the time that he had left.*

MICHAEL

"I'm getting out of here."

*The T.D.B. shrieks an alarm and reads in big bold red letters
"Error. Timeline disruption".*

MICHAEL CONT'D

*Shaking his head in terror at being stuck with no way out, he
panics:*

"What the fuck! Oh no no no no no no!"

*He tries to punch in the numbers again. The T.D.B. reads
"Error. Timeline disruption". Realization hits him like a solid
punch from a heavy weight boxer. When he killed the soldier in*

---

the corridor just after entering the bunker he invariably altered the future.

Yells can be heard getting closer to the room. The battle cry of many angry Russian soldiers can be heard storming the halls of the underground bunker. Knowing that he cannot get back to his own place in the strings of time, fear grips Michael's heart. The yells of the soldiers grow louder as they make their way through the halls. Mind askew, Michael franticly punches in random numbers. The blue glow suffuses him and he disappears. Seconds later the Russian soldiers storm the room with guns drawn. They find the bodies of Adolf Hitler and Eva Braun slumped in their chairs and they celebrate.

CHAPTER 5

EXT. STORMY NIGHT- FRANCE

The black sky crackles with lightning as the rain falls in sheets of icy darts. The small town is illuminated by the thunderous crackle of lightning. The blinding flashes reflects off of the rain causing the sky to glow with an electric purple haze. An area above a small house shimmers as the fabric of space distorts and Michael drops out of the vortex onto the angled roof. The steep angle of the roof causes him to roll towards its edge. Michael grabs the nearest thing to keep from falling off. The rain and thunder of the violent storm covers the clatter made by his graceless plunge through time. He pulls himself up and lies on the roof. He looks at the date on the T.D.B.. His brows furrow in frustrated rage when he sees that it reads, Domremy, France 1410, Dec. 28.

Michael's hands drop to his side as he screams in and pounds his head against the shingles of the roof. He lies there regretting ever putting on the time travel device. After a long period has passed, he sits up to look at his surroundings and to try to get a sense of where he might go to escape the deluge. The steep roofs of the homes and structures of the village lay in a sort of uniformity that it doesn't seem real. The total darkness of the night is alien to him. No electricity, street lamps, or neon signs to combat the pitch black of the night. A yellow orange glow seeps out of the shutter slats in many of the windows. He can see smoke drift lazily into the air as it escapes the chimneys.

He makes his way down to the oversaturated, muddy ground and spies a barn in the distance. Picking his way carefully through the streets, Michael tries to step on the wooden planks strewn all about to keep his feet from sinking into the waste that seeps into the earth.

INT. BARN

The smell of animal manure is pungent and overpowering to the senses. The hay and dried grass lay in neat piles about the staging area of the barn, whilst the pigs pinned on the other side scamper over each other squealing and snorting. Michael tries once again to punch in the numbers to his own time and gets the same Error message. In a rage Michael slams his fist into a wall knocking farming tools off their nailed posts and onto the dirt and straw covered ground. After some time had passed and some long inner reflection, exhaustion takes hold of Michael and he falls asleep under a pile of hay.

INT. NEXT MORNING IN THE BARN

The next morning, the sounds of animals and people can be heard outside, as the small village has come to life while the weary traveler slept. Luckily the farmer who tends to the pigs *has not yet come in to the barn to check his stock. Hanging next to the main door, Michael finds a cloak and wraps it around his shoulders in a poor attempt to disguise his unfamiliar clothes and blend with the people of the village as much as possible. He makes his way out of the barn, through the muck field and on to the street. There he finds his feet firmly planted in a huge pile of horse manure. He nods in sarcastic approval despite having permanently ruined his boots. Michael takes a deep breath. He notices that the air feels denser and cleaner than what he is used to.*

Villagers walk alongside their mule carts advertising their wares and produce, though they don't have much to spare. Some of the small houses have children running circles around them. Other folks mill about greeting friends and family members, but most glare at the strange man standing in a pile of shit. Noticing that he sticks out like a poorly hammered nail, Michael starts to walk away but is almost run over by half a dozen soldiers on horseback dressed in light plate armor.

EXT. IN THE VILLAGE

The soldiers move into the town. Michael steps out of the way like so many others in the village. People begin to bring gifts to the men, hoping to save themselves or family from persecution and death. Some of the men take the loaves of bread and baskets of fruit as they kick the people giving it to them. Michael can't help but feel sorry for these people.

The lightly armored men come to a stop in front of a small shack. He can see the men talking amongst themselves before a crowd gathers and obscures his view. He joins the gathering crowd, pushing his way through the dense mass of bodies to a position that is more suitable for a closer look at what is going on.

MICHAEL

"What's happening?"

The middle aged man that answers has short cropped hair with a day's worth of hair growth on his face. His thick brown clothes are tightly wrapped to insulate his body from the cold morning air. Capron jerks his head to see who is speaking and knits his brows at the odd man standing next to him. The man looks strange to Capron, but then again he knows that these are strange times.

CAPRON

"Your English is not very… It's odd my friend, but to answer your question, it is judgment."

Michael looks on. The guards lumber off their mounts and gather in front of the flimsy wood door. Two of the men draw their swords while another kicks in the door to the small house and they rush in. A struggle can be heard. A woman screams as something like clay or glass crashes to the floor. The men drag out an old frail man who is still dressed in his underclothes. A crimson trickle flows from the side of his head and spills onto his dirty white shirt. They toss the old man onto the backside of a horse then one of men smashes the pommel of his weapon into the side of the elderly man's head knocking him out. They tie the unconscious man to the back of the horse and head back inside the small dwelling. The woman's wailing screams penetrate the stillness of the terror gripped villagers. Some begin to cry as they take hold of their loved ones and scamper toward their homes. After some time, the men drag the young woman out the house. Her disheveled hair hangs over her face concealing her blackened eyes. Her brown gown is torn partially revealing one of her breasts. Her face is bruised and bloody from the abuse inflicted by the savage men restraining her.

GUARD

"You have been charged with the crime of heresy and have been called to stand trial."

The woman desperately pleads with the guards. They just smile and laugh at the young dark haired girl then slap her.

MARY

"No! There has been some mistake! You have the wrong people. We are faithful."

GUARD

"We shall see."

The doomed family is taken away. The other villagers rush in once the guards have left and raid the tiny house, for they know the small family won't be coming back.

CAPRON

"Those poor damned fools. There will not be a trial. More innocent people dragged off to their deaths and for what? A Church whose insecurity in its message has led the lambs to the slaughter in order to secure its power over the people."

MICHAEL

"Why didn't anybody help them?"

CAPRON

"If they did, they would be labeled a conspirator with those who are branded heretics. Do you expect others to doom themselves to torture or worse? I think not my friend. Besides, I didn't see you dashing in to be the hero."

MICHAEL

"I just got here... It's still not right. Why won't the people rise up in revolt?"

The cynicism behind the man's laugh wounds Michael. The man shakes his head as he turns and walks away.

CAPRON

"That kind of thinking will get you killed, my friend."

Michael walks over to the ransacked house and looks inside. The two were in the middle of a meager breakfast. The small table that once held their clay bowls lies on its side with one leg broken. The bowls that held their porridge had been shattered and its contents lay in a cooling mess all over the wood floor. A pile of straw that must have served as their bed lay scattered in the corner.

MICHAEL

"Just a pot to piss in. Those poor bastards."

Turning his attention to Capron, Michael jogs to catch up to him. The eccentric man seems to be speed walking to where ever he needs to go. Something must be wrong.

MICHAEL CONT'D

"Hey! Wait a minute."

Michael begins to run in order to catch up to Capron, who is doing his best not to slip in the mud. The crowd parts as if touching Capron will stain them forever. The soft earth squelches under their feet as they trek through the mud and animal waste.

CAPRON

"What is it, libre penseur?"

(Free thinker)?

MICHAEL

"I haven't eaten in a while…"

CAPRON

Capron cuts him off mid-sentence:

"I see, and you want me to just hand some coins over to you? That is not an option for me, penseur."

(Thinker)

MICHAEL

"Uh, no. I was wondering if you had some food. I can work it off if need be."

CAPRON

"Nothing comes without a cost. What is it you can do for me?"

MICHAEL

"I don't know. What do you need?"

CAPRON

"You speak very strangely. You are not from around here, are you?"

MICHAEL

"No I'm not."

Capron stops mid stride, sharply turning his body to look Michael up and down. He's obviously trying to figure out who and where the stranger had come from. Finding no real answers that he can solidly prove as fact, he smiles and shakes

*his head. Capron puts his hand out to greet Michael. The two
men clasp hands and shake.*

CAPRON

"I am Capron."

MICHAEL

"I'm Michael."

CAPRON

"Good to meet you, Michael. When you have figured out
what you can do for me, come find me."

*Michael stops walking while Capron continues to walk away.
Not knowing what the man actually needs, Michael looks back
at the ransacked house and has a thought. In times like these,
some people may need protection and he's pretty sure that this
sly character could use someone with his particular skill set.*

MICHAEL

"I can fight!"

*Capron turns around with renewed interest in the strange man
and carefully looks him over. Michael can tell that the man is
seriously weighing his options. Capron takes a deep breath as
he has made his decision.*

CAPRON

"I knew there was something you could do, penseur.
Come with me. "

CHAPTER 6

EXT. FRONT DOOR CAPRON'S HOUSE

Michael follows the man calling himself Capron to a house on the other side of the small village. The home is larger than the others surrounding it, but not by much. Capron moves to open the door then pauses considering something, then turns back to Michael.

CAPRON

"Now, don't mind my sister. She can be, how do you say? A little crazy."

Capron smiles, turns around, takes a steadying breath, then he opens the wooden door and they walk inside.

INT. THE HOUSE OF CAPRON

The pleasant aroma of a boiling stew fills the small home and speaks sweet nothings to Michael's empty stomach. A woman stands by the hearth peeling potatoes. Her dark curly hair rests atop her head wrapped in a black scarf. The embers from the fire drift into the air and fall back down ash grey. Black soot rests on the woman's face and clothes yet, her red dress is cleaner than most of the women he had seen in the village. Some of the strings to her corset are broken and held together in little knots.

For a moment she ignores her brother as he walks into the house, only when the second set of footsteps enter the dwelling does she tear herself away from her cooking.

MAGDALINA

Turns around fury plain on her face:

"qui la baise est-ce? "

(Who the fuck is that?)

CAPRON

"Il s'agit d'un nouvel ami. Il a faim."

(He's a new friend. He's hungry.)

MICHAEL

"She's upset."

CAPRON

"Oh no no. She just says that you are handsome. That's all."

Capron turns back to his fierce sister a little aggravated, yet it only shows in his tone of voice.

CAPRON

"Tais-toi et faire ressortir la nourriture. "

(Just shut up and bring out the food.)

The woman violently waves a big wooden spoon around in their general direction as she screams in her native tongue.

MAGDALINA

"Vous avez deux bras et les jambes qui ne sont pas encore brisés. Recevez-vous et nourrir votre parasite. "

(You have two arms and legs that aren't broken yet. Get it yourself and feed your stray.)

She turns to Michael and calmly addresses him. Her cold eyes betray her kind tone in her words. She shoots an angry glare at her brother.

MAGDALINA

"Bonjour. Sit and my idiot brother will give you some food."

Michael sits down in a simple wooden chair amazed and a bit amused at how abruptly she changed her demeanor. He looks around to see that there isn't much to the small house. There is only one bed and a rolled up mat next to it. The small chamber pot sits in a corner next to a bowl filled with water. The smell of the stew cooking over a fire makes Michaels stomach rumble. The meats and potatoes boiling in the broth, fills the tiny house with its intoxicating aroma.

MICHAEL

"Thank you."

She smiles at Michael, and then turns around to her brother whispering.

MAGDALINA

"Pourquoi avez-vous amené ici? "

(Why did you bring him here?)

Capron turns his head and smiles at Michael. He then awkwardly if not woodenly turns back to his sister to continue their whispered conversation.

CAPRON

"Il dit qu'il peut se battre et vous êtes plaint toujours traîner avec moi tout le temps. "

(He says he can fight and you're always complaining about hanging out with me all the time.)

Pausing from the fiery but hushed conversation, the hard yet, beautiful woman turns her head and smiles awkwardly at the stranger in her home, then turns back to her brother still whispering. Michael begins to worry about the possible direction the conversation could be heading. If they have to smile like that in between view points, it must not be going good.

MAGDALINA

"Vous devriez avoir mis quelqu'un qui a au moins l'argent. Il sent comme de la merde de porc. "

(You should have brought someone who at least has money. He smells like pig shit.)

They both turn their heads to look at Michael. They both smile awkwardly at him. Michael looks back at them with his eyes wide. He's watched this movie before and he knows that it usually doesn't end well for the person left out of the loop. They turn around to continue their conversation.

CAPRON

"Super, maintenant il pense sans doute que nous allons lui ou quelque chose manger. "

(Great, now he probably thinks we are going to eat him or something.)

They turn around and present the food to Michael. Capron beams at Michael and nods his head at the steaming food silently letting his guest know that he should eat.

MICHAEL

Eyes opened really wide and unsure:

"Please, don't eat me."

CAPRON

Capron laughs and glares at his sister:

"We are not savages, though, my sister is very good at convincing some people that we are. My sister and I tend to disagree on many things and this was one of them. We did not mean to make you worry."

MAGDALINA

"What my brother does not seem to understand, is that he just can't bring home vagabonds and expect them not to steal or not return the kindness."

MAGDALINA CONT'D

"So what about you? What is your name?"

MICHAEL

"I'm Michael. I'm just hungry."

Taking a bite out of some bread and placing a steaming cup on the table in front of her, Magdalina sits in a chair. Aggravation clear in her body language, she leans forward, and eyes narrowed. She folds her arms around her drink. Michael can feel the tension hanging in the air between them.

MAGDALINA

"So, Michael I'm just hungry, I know you are not from around here. You have no money yet, you have that gauntlet on your arm. The buttons on your coat are silver. What do you do? Are you a thief?"

Michael covers up the drift band with his sleeve, inwardly wincing at his carelessness. He highly doubts that they would guess his origins, but best not to leave that to chance.

CAPRON

"Are you on the run? An exile perhaps?"

MICHAEL

Michael's eyes tear up as the reality of his impossible situation washes over him:

"There is no easy way to explain this, but I'm not a thief; I'm a lost traveler."

The siblings look at each other in confusion. Magdalina raises one eyebrow at her brother as if to say, "Horse shit".

CAPRON

"I know my way around this world, there is no need to worry. Where are you from?"

MAGDALINA

Taking a sip of some warm liquid:

"Escroc. "

(Con artist)

CAPRON

"J'ai vu les larmes d'un escroc. Enfer, je les ai pleuré moi-même. Cela se sent réel."

(I have seen the tears of a con artist. Hell, I have cried them myself. This feels real.)

MAGDALINA

Shrugs and takes another bite of bread:

"Très bon escroc. "

(Very good con artist.)

MICHAEL

"I'm sorry. This is something you don't need to worry about."

Michael begins to eat. Magdalina sits back and examines her strange guest. He can feel her judging him by every small move he makes.

MAGDALINA

"You don't seem like the rest of the travelers that we have seen come through here. That gauntlet on your arm is too rich for a vagabond like yourself. Where did you come from? If you are going to stay in my home, you will tell me or you can leave."

Looking at his sister with a pleading expression, Capron tries to ease her mood. He knows that they could use a friend in these dire times.

CAPRON

"There's no need to be hard."

MICHAEL

"No, it's fine. It's only fair. I can tell you where I come from, but I know you will not believe me."

There is a knock at the door. The stern woman holds up one finger, forestalling Michael's tale. She pushes herself up out of her chair, strolls over to the front door and cracks it open to see who stands on the other side. Capron nods at Michael and fidgets in his seat nervously.

CAPRON

"You can tell us later."

Magdalina opens the door and a lady who is not much older than her is holding a basket of fruit. Magdalina smiles warmly at her and they embrace.

MAGDALINA

"Isabelle!"

ISABELLE

Smiling:

"I come with treats."

Isabelle walks in and stops when she spots Michael sitting at the table.

ISABELLE CONT'D

"Oh! I didn't know you had a guest."

Capron and Michael stand to greet Isabelle.

CAPRON

"Isabelle this is Michael. Michael this is Isabelle Romée"

Isabelle bows her head to greet the strange young man. Her questioning eyes meet Magdalina's.

CAPRON CONT'D

"He is a new friend of ours."

MAGDALINA

Leans over to Isabelle and whispers:

"Il est un vagabond."

(He is a vagabond)

ISABELLE

She leans over to Magdalina and whispers:

"Pourquoi fait-il sentir comme de la merde?"

(Why does he smell like shit?)

Magdalina shrugs, then walks back over to the table and sits.

Capron pulls up a seat for Isabelle, but she sits in Capron's seat next to Magdalina. Isabelle seems confused as to why her friend would be entertaining such a strange guest. Capron and Michael sit. The name of the woman rings a bell in Michael's head, but cannot recall its importance. Michael looks down at his bowl to keep from staring at the woman.

MAGDALINA

"We were just discussing where Michael came from."

CAPRON

Cutting off his sister's words:

"So Isabelle did you break any young hearts lately?"

ISABELLE

"Contrary of what you believe Capron, I'm not like the women you associate with during your free time."

Michael continues to eat while watching the trio interact with each other. Outwardly he projects an aura of impassivity, but inwardly he thinks the entire situation is comical.

CAPRON

"Surely you must have your eyes set on some young man. Who is the lucky dog?"

The truth was that she did have eyes for a man, a man she had known for some time, married and bore children with. Magdalina knew of Isabelle's life and they were both perfectly content with letting Capron dream perversely.

MAGDALINA

"Just because you are a dog, does not mean that every man is a dog."

Michael chuckles a bit at her assertion.

CAPRON

Looking at Michael with a smile:

"What's this? I thought you were on my side."

Isabelle giggles at the two men.

ISABELLE

"It seems Michael knows how to pick his battles. A wise man."

MICHAEL

Chuckles again:

"I don't know about wise, but I do know when not to argue with a lady."

MAGDALINA

She smiles, grabs an apple out of Isabelle's basket and takes a huge bite:

"Hmm."

ISABELLE

"Did you hear about, Mary and her father?"

Magdalina perks up in attention at her friend's words. Capron shifts in his seat. He was hoping to gently break the news to his sister.

CAPRON

"Michael and I were there."

MAGDALINA

"What happened? Are they ok?"

MICHAEL

"Some guards took them away."

Hearing of the poor family's fate, Magdalina's entire mood shifts from aggravated and annoyed to extremely frightened. Capron places his hand over hers in an attempt to calm her worry.

MAGDALINA

"You don't think?"

CAPRON

"I don't know, but we must plan for the worst. "

Magdalina reaches over the table to smack her brother as her anger crests.

MAGDALINA

"Why didn't you say anything Cul?!"

Michael lifts his head at the sound of a hand colliding with flesh. He doesn't know the significance of such events, but he knows that they are not good and this is why Capron has changed his mind so easily when they first met.

CAPRON

"I didn't want to alarm you."

ISABELLE

Worried for her friends:

"Is everything ok?"

MAGDALINA

Getting up from the table:

"Isabelle you should get going."

ISABELLE

Being escorted out of the house by Magdalina:

"Are you going to be ok? What is going on?"

MAGDALINA

"Everything is fine, but for now you must go. Thank you for the apples."

MICHAEL

Looking at Capron:

"You knew them personally, didn't you?"

CAPRON

"Oui. They are our cousins."

Magdalina, lets Isabelle out of the house. Her nerves were high strung before and now they've snapped leaving her in a state of panic. She knew they should have left the country with the rest of their family when they had the chance but, she and her brother did not realize that trouble would find them so quickly. For once she was glad her brother brought someone home who at least claimed to know something about fighting. The man looked capable but looks can be deceiving. She only hopes that they would have enough time to get away.

MAGDALINA

"Capron, why did you not tell me about this? They will come for us."

CAPRON

Gets up to comfort his sister:

"Everything will be fine."

Capron looks over at Michael with a pained expression in his eyes. The poor man regrets getting Michael mixed into their bad situation.

"I am sorry my friend, but you must go. I'm sorry to have put you in this situation."

MICHAEL

"There is no reason for you to be sorry. The situation I'm in is the fault of my own ignorance. You gave me food. What do you need me to do?"

Magdalina continues to cry into her brother's shoulder as he holds her.

CAPRON

"I don't think that there is anything you can do against the Inquisition. They will just kill you too."

Horses can be heard in the distance entering the village. Not being able stomach the site of another pair of beings savaged, Michael makes his decision.

MICHAEL

"You and your sister should get the hell out of here. I will stall them for you."

Eyes filled with fear and hope she looks at Michael in disbelief. Now she can see the man in a completely different light.

MAGDALINA

"Merci."

(Thank you)

Capron grabs a small sack then begins to stuff it with cloths and food. Magdalina regrets ever mistreating this man. Magdalina finds new respect for Michael, who was now risking his life to save her and her brother. Magdalina swallows her pride.

MAGDALINA CONT'D

Walks up to Michael:

"I am sorry to have treated you so harshly. I know what you are now."

Capron double checks the small house for useful things before moving close to Magdalina.

MAGDALINA CONT'D

"Un tuteur"

(A guardian)

Capron takes Magdalina by the hand and hugs Michael then heads for the exit. Magdalina glances back at Michael before they slip out the back.

The rhythmic pounding of the horses get closer. By the sound of their hooves in the mud, they must be around the corner. Michael pulls a chair up to face the door, looks at the T.D.B. and breathes deeply. Michael pulls out his gun, his A.X.L. and sits in the chair. His deep breaths are an attempt to calm his spastic nerves. He knows he can't go back to his time, so he wants to do something helpful even if it is reckless. He knows that he will alter the future drastically if he kills the guards headed his way. He knows that there is a possibility that he may even erase a few friends, but he can't let innocent people die when there could be something he could have done to prevent it.

CHAPTER 7

EXT. GRASS FIELD

Capron and Magdalina run through the field beyond the small homes of the village. The tall grass whips against their arms, neatly cutting the exposed flesh and impeding their progress.

MAGDALINA

"They are going to kill him!"

INT. HOUSE OF CAPRON

Inside the small house the thumping hooves of the horses can be heard just outside the door. Michael can hear the men climbing down from their mounts and marching toward the door. Michael taps his finger against the barrel of gun, waiting for the armed men to kick in the door.

EXT. GRASS FIELD

Out in the field the siblings make their escape. The edge of the forest is so close that they can smell the damp vegetation on the air.

CAPRON

"He offered to help and besides, he said he could fight well."

INT. HOUSE OF CAPRON

Michael turns on his A.X.L. The lasers heat up and form a blade of purple swirling fire. Michael takes one last deep breath.

EXT. GRASSY FIELD

Out in the field the tree line can be seen. The siblings make a mad dash for it.

EXT. THE FRONT DOOR OF CAPRON'S HOUSE

The door bursts open. Michael jumps to his feet. The guards stop in confusion and awe. They obviously expected to find the siblings, who would have been easy prey for them, but instead they find this hooded man whose body screams intimidation. The hood covers most of his face adding to the soldier's dismay. The steel swords that were leveled at Michael begin to droop in the hands of the men wielding them.

EXT. GRASS FIELD

The siblings reach the edge of the forest, hop over the thick bush and vanish into the dense vegetation. Their lungs burn as they try to take more air in. They both want to stop, but the adrenaline coursing through their bodies won't let them. Magdalina hikes up her dress to keep from tripping over it as she leaps over the protruding roots of an old tree.

INT. HOUSE OF CAPRON

The guards and Michael are locked in a standoff. The hapless squad stands frozen in confusion and fear. Michael becomes impatient with the men. He was counting on them making the first move so he would be free of guilt when he defended himself. When they didn't attack he threw all pretenses of this being purely self defense out of his mind.

MICHAEL

"You and your sanctimonious Church judge and spill the blood of the innocent. Well, I have already judged you and determined your fate."

Michael looks up at them so that they can see the rage that is etched in his features.

MICHAEL CONT'D

"When I'm done with you not even God will recognize your mangled faces. Are you ready?"

GUARD

Frozen in fear, he only mutters.

"Cher seigneur"

(Dear Lord)

Michael lunges past the closest guard who flinched at the movement, then he shoots the second guard and spins full circle to slice through the first man. Michael's arm comes over his head and cuts the next guard just off center, down his body. The two halves fall apart.

Michael raises his gun and shoots another armed guard in the face. The villagers jump when the loud gun goes off. One of the men tries to slash at Michael with his sword, but Michael cuts through the steel and part of the guard's head goes flying off. Michael spins around and points his gun directly in the face of the last guard. The last guard swallows deeply. The trigger is pulled.

Pieces of the guards are everywhere and Michael stands in the chaos. The growing crowd of people gather but keep their distance from the man with the burning sword. Some cry while others fall to their knees in absolute awe of the man standing before them. For a moment, Michael doesn't seem to understand.

OLD WOMAN

"Cette épée de feu? Il sera Michel Archange."

(That sword of fire? It be Michael, the Archangel.)

The old woman falls to her knees.

"Are you here to save us?"

Michael looks at the old woman. He spots Isabelle moving through the crowd of awestruck people. Isabelle looks like she has seen the face of God.

MICHAEL

Looks back at the old woman and helps her stand:

"Only you can save yourself."

Michael notices there are guards down the road. They have seen what he's done. They turn around and head back the way they came. The villagers slowly move forward, never taking their eyes from the man with the fiery sword. Isabelle walks up to Michael in wonder. Her watering eyes are like sparkling diamonds as she places her hand on his face. She gasps as if all the wind had been stolen from her body then she faints. Michael catches the girl. He'd never actually seen a woman swoon before.

CHAPTER 8

INT. CASTLE

Voices can be heard talking behind large double doors. The Pope John the XXIII, who is known to be ruthless in all matters, is defined by his cruelty and has been dubbed the Anti-Pope. His hooked nose and thinning brows only add to the menace his physical presence emanates. The two men in the room cower before the Pope. The tension is palpable and it makes the knights shake in their greaves.

POPE JOHN XXIII

In an almost incoherent rage:

"Incompetent fools!"

The guards rest on their knees addressing the Pope. They dare not look the old man in the eyes. Their minds race with thoughts of fear.

GUARD

"Your Eminence, he wielded the sword of the Arch Angels. He said we shed the blood of innocence."

The Pope lifts the head of the guard with a gentle forefinger then slaps him. The large rings on his hand gouges a bloody furrow in the man's cheek.

POPE JOHN XXIII

Enraged:

"I am the voice of God! I know who is innocent and who is not!"

GUARD 3

"He... he had the flaming sword of the Arch Angel."

POPE JOHN XXIII

The Pope signals for another guard:

"Go and fetch me some pitch."

The guard makes haste to comply with the Pope's orders. The Pope walks around the cowering men looking down at them with spiteful scorn etched on his face.

POPE JOHN XXIII CONT'D

"When you looked upon him, did you see the grace of God?"

COWERING GUARD

"I was frightened your Holiness."

POPE JOHN XXIII

Leaning forward into the face of the frightened man:

"You felt fear in the face of this so called, "Angel" of the Lord. You don't know fear. Not yet."

The Pope curls his fingers around the tip of his staff and pulls to reveal a long slender blade.

POPE JOHN XXIII

Looking at the sword:

"Straight and true is my sword. It doesn't bend or compromise itself for any man. It has served my predecessors very well."

The two guards glance at each other and share an uneasy look.

COWERING GUARD

"Your..."

He is interrupted with a gesture by the Pope. The other guard returns with a small barrel of pitch. The Pope extends his free hand in joy that the other guard has come back so quickly.

POPE JOHN XXIII

"Just in time. Thank you my child."

The guard kneels as he presents the small barrel of black oil to the Pope. The old man dips the slender sword into the barrel.

POPE JOHN XXIII CONT'D

"This is a very important time for the Church."

COWERING GUARD

"We did not know what to do, Holy Father!"

POPE JOHN XXIII

Pulling the sword out of the barrel and tipping its blade upward so that its entire length is covered in the dark slick substance:

"You are a true reflection of your people…"

The men watch confused, he positions the sword over a candle and the sword burst into flames.

POPE JOHN XXIII CONT'D

"Weak. That is why England thinks it can run all over you and continue this damned war. I will not allow your weak will to get in the way of our Lord."

Mocking the men, the Pope puts his hand up to his mouth in surprise as the flames dance along the length of the sword.

POPE JOHN XXIII CONT'D

"Oh look at that. My sword is on fire."

The Pope thrust the sword into one of the kneeling men as he looks at the other with cruel intent:

"I must be an Angel!"

EXT. THE CASTLE WALLS

Anguished screams fill the halls of the large castle, escaping out into the courtyard through the windows and murder holes located throughout the structure. The guards patrolling the grounds do their best to ignore the screams as they go about their duties.

INT. HOUSE OF CAPRON AND MAGDALINA

Isabelle wakes up inside the home of Capron and Magdalina to find that night has fallen. All the people in the village respected Michael's plea for privacy and retreated to their homes and shacks. The crackling of the fire draws the weary time traveler into deep thought about the actions that had lead him to this point. He can't help but hate the situation, yet he is unable to find a solution.

Isabelle sits up in the small bed, her eyes never leaving the visage of Michael, who is sitting by the fire. He's pressing the buttons on the T.D.B. trying to find a way back home. He is frustrated when he receives another error message. He hits a wall.

ISABELLE

Frightened:

"Eh..."

Michael looks at her.

MICHAEL

"I'm sorry, I woke you."

Isabelle pushes herself off the cot and walks over to Michael. She kneels down before him and to his dismay she kisses his hand.

ISABELLE

"I had no idea."

Michael looks down at the woman confused.

MICHAEL

"No idea about what?"

She looks up at Michael with a teary, yet hopeful expression.

ISABELLE

"You are Michael."

Realizing what she means, Michael begins to shake his head in protest. Before he can react Isabelle jumps to her feet and hugs the bewildered man.

MICHAEL

"I..."

ISABELLE

"I knew you would come and save us from the tyranny."

She looks him in the eyes:

"I almost gave up faith. I was beginning to think that God had forsaken us."

MICHAEL

Feeling guilty:

"I am here to help."

ISABELLE

Looks around:

"Where are Capron and Magdalina?"

MICHAEL

"They left in fear of the Inquisition. Do you know where they might have gone?"

The star struck woman thinks for a moment then snaps her fingers.

ISABELLE

"There is an old farm house on the outskirts of the village that only we know of. They may have gone there."

MICHAEL

"Show me."

Isabella heads toward the back exit. The playful way she skips out the doorway makes Michael smile.

EXT. GRASS FIELD

The moon light shines down on the long blades of grass as they sway in the gentle breeze.

ISABELLE

"What is God like? Is he old?"

MICHAEL

Laughing:

"Is God old? Isabelle you have read the Bible?"

ISABELLE

"I can't read, but it has been read to me."

MICHAEL

"Ok then. I don't think so. Have you heard the part where they describe God as vengeful, jealous, loving and forgiving?"

ISABELLE

"Of course I have. What does that have to do with my question?"

MICHAEL

"I guess what I am saying is; who do you know with those traits?"

She stops walking and looks at Michael with weary

consternation in her eyes.

ISABELLE

"Hmm… My mom, uh Magdalina… Are you saying that God is a woman?!"

MICHAEL

"God could be a woman, but I don't really know. In the Bible they all seem to be describing the personality traits of a woman, but they refer to God as a male. My mother was the only one, I was ever sure who loved me while she punished me."

ISABELLE

Walking again:

"What do you mean? God COULD be a woman? Have you actually met God?"

MICHAEL

"No, I've never met God. I came pretty close once, but no dice.

ISABELLE

"No dice? So, you have never met God? That does not surprise me. God created everything. It must be tiring. You know?"

Isabelle looks up at the stars with hopeful optimism filling her body and adding a bounce to her step:

"You know the Church has burned people who spoke of a different dogma than their own. They say that they are doing the work of God and stamping out heresy. I like the idea of God being a woman, though. I mean we were given free will, yet the Church tells us it is a sin to use it and if you do they kill you. It just seems so wrong to kill someone because they are different."

MICHAEL

"Amen sister. Someone can tell you about God, but that is only their interpretation. You need to learn all you can to open your own eyes to your reality."

A twig snaps in the darkness. Michael and Isabelle stop. Michael draws his gun. Isabelle looks around in the direction of the noise. The night conceals most of their surroundings making it hard to see. Michael focuses on the tree line scanning it for movement.

MICHAEL CONT'D

"Isabelle, get low."

They sink into the tall grass. Michael can see a stray dog walking out of the forest. They let out a sigh of relief and continue walking.

CHAPTER 9

INT. THE POPE'S CHAMBERS

Inside the Pope's chambers he talks with a mysterious man in dark hooded robes. The man speaks in hushed tones, but it is almost as if the man speaks directly to the mind of Pope John the XXIII. The aging man sits at a large candle lit desk.

POPE JOHN XXIII

"How would you have me handle this situation, my Lord?"

The man's details are lost in the miasma of darkness that envelopes the corner of the room. The light from the fireplace occasionally illuminates parts of his body revealing only the man's thick dark robes. The long candles nearest to the man flicker as if dancing in a strong wind with every word that leaves his lips.

MAN

"This man must not make it out of France alive. I don't care how many men you use, exterminate this bug."

POPE JOHN XXIII

"I will get rid of him at once, my Lord."

MAN

"I will not accept failure."

The man fades into the darkness. The candles flicker violently for a moment. The Pope summons his guards.

GUARD

"How may we serve you, your Holiness?"

Pope John leans back in his chair, his eyes are dark with distain.

POPE JOHN XXIII

"Get me your best men and find this so called, Angel. Bring him to me."

The guard bows his head and leaves. The rattling of chains can be heard in a dark corner of the Pope's chambers. The battered young woman who had been taken the day before cowers in fear while pressing herself against the wall.

The Pope looks at her and smiles. He rises from his seat and walks over to the squirming woman. Her body trembles and her eyes water as the sadistic Pope approaches her.

MARY

"Pe... pe... please. No more."

The Pope pulls on a rope attached to a pulley that is tied to a bar that separates her ankles until she is suspended in the air upside down. He ties the rope off to hold her in place. He grabs a knife from a drawer and walks up to her.

The woman begins to cry uncontrollably. The evil man caresses her face and wipes away her tears. The woman squirms tying to free herself, but the bonds that clasp her hands behind her back are tight and will not budge. She shrieks in horror as the Pope leans in close, and licks her face.

POPE JOHN XXIII

"Your tears bring me comfort, my child. Through your fear, I realize the dream of our Lord; A one world order. I see his power in your pain. You should be honored to have been chosen to be a representative of the people. You will be the first of many to tremble before our Lord."

He takes a deep breath and places his hands on his chest and exhales as he looks at the ceiling in a trance like state. His eyes roll back into their sockets and he begins to pant like a wild animal. He lifts the knife to his lips and kisses the blade.

MARY

She can barely form words she is crying so much:

"Please."

The Pope looks down at her, fury burning in his eyes for disrupting his sense of nirvana, and cuts at her face with a quick jab of his knife. The woman screams. The Pope screams

---

with her, mocking her terror, then he proceeds to slice a piece of her thigh off and eat it. The woman looks on screaming in horror as the deranged man eats her flesh.

POPE JOHN XXIII

Insanely mad:

"That is it, my child! Feed me your soul!"

The Pope reaches over to his desk and grabs a dull brass candle holder. The ornate design of the holder incorporates jagged edges all around its shaft. He pulls out the candle and holds the flame to the screaming woman's hair. He smiles grimly as he watches the strands sizzle and burn. The woman shakes and screams as the flames lick her face, burning her eyebrows. The Pope pants in ecstasy, then he sticks the knife between his teeth and grabs the woman by the neck with his free hand and begins to strangle her.

He takes the ornately decorated candle holder and rams it between her legs. The woman screams in agony as the deranged Pope thrusts it in and out of her. The woman tries desperately to break free of the ropes and chains that bind her. The shackles around her ankles peel the skin back in bloody slivers, exposing muscle and bone. Savagely, the Pope continues to defile her. Servants just outside the doors and in the halls look to the floor in shame. The blood curdling screams of the woman fills the castle.

CHAPTER 10

EXT. DEEP IN THE WOODS

Michael and Isabelle come to an old house in the forest. The wooden structure appears to be falling apart. Lush emerald vines and vegetation cover most of the house and its windows. A faint light can be seen inside.

INT. OLD SHACK

ISABELLE

"This is it. They must have come here."

Isabelle runs up to the door and swings it open:

"Hey guys look who I've brought with me."

The old house appears empty except for the lantern burning on a barrel near the back door.

ISABELLE CONT'D

"'ello?"

Michael scans for movement. A floor board begins to move up and to the side. Capron pokes his head out with a big smile on his face.

CAPRON

"Bonjour les amis!"

(Hello friends!)

Capron climbs out of the hole in the floor, then he reaches back in to help his sister, Magdalina climb out.

MAGDALINA

"Haven't you heard ladies go first? You are such a jerk."

CAPRON

"I'm not your personal stepping stool woman."

Magdalina and Capron climb out of the hole. Once she's out she wraps her arms around Michael's neck and kisses him on the cheek.

MAGDALINA

"Michael, Isabelle you made it! This calls for a celebration."

ISABELLE

"You missed one hell of a show!"

CAPRON

"Well, it must have been good to have you using language like that young lady."

Capron turns to Michael and puts his hand on his shoulder.

CAPRON CONT'D

"I am forever in your debt my friend. Once this is over, you can have all the food you want."

MAGDALINA

Looking at Michael:

"Did the guards run like the cowards they are?"

ISABELLE

"The ones that never made it to your front door did. As for the others… there wasn't much left of them to run away."

CAPRON

Looks at Michael in shock:

"What did you do to them?"

ISABELLE

"The people in the village looked on as the guards broke down your door and then froze when they saw Michael there, waiting for them. His fiery sword at his side and his boom stick thing in the other."

Capron and Magdalina look on humored.

ISABELLE CONT'D

"He asked them if they were ready to die and then he just."

Isabelle begins acting out the one sided battle between Michael and the guards with a stick in her hand and pointing her fingers in the shape of a gun to mimic Michael's Equalizer while making sound effects with her mouth.

MAGDALINA

Laughing at what Isabelle is doing:

"Isabelle, stop telling impossible stories. What really happened Michael?"

MICHAEL

"I thinks she explained it very accurately."

CAPRON

"Where did you get the sword? And what is a boom stick?"

MICHAEL

He shows them the handle to the A.X.L.

"Well I've always had my sword."

MAGDALINA

"That's so small. How do you keep a sword in there?"

He shows them the Equalizer.

CAPRON

Surprised:

"What the hell is that?"

MICHAEL

"My 'boom stick'. The Equalizer."

CAPRON

"What does it do?"

ISABELLE

"It makes things explode."

Capron's jaw drops.

MAGDALINA

"Forget about his big stick. I want to know how you have a sword in that little thing."

Michael turns on the A.X.L. and their eyes grow wide in wonder. Capron rubs his eyes to ensure that the things he is seeing are indeed real. The lasers begin to swirl giving it the flaming whirlwind effect. Isabelle looks at Michael with a big smile.

ISABELLE

"He is Michael, and he is here to help us."

The siblings faint. Amused at their reactions, Michael and Isabelle exchange a small smile. Michael knew what they meant every time they referred to him by his first name, but he didn't see a need to correct them or dash their hopes.

MICHAEL

"Get some sleep. We will have a big day ahead of us tomorrow."

Michael deactivates his weapon, then finds a seat next to the door and closes his eyes, attempting to rest. Isabelle lays next the siblings and tries to fall asleep, but her excitement keeps her awake for hours.

INT. OLD BARN

The next morning Michael wakes to Magdalina, Capron and Isabelle standing over him apparently watching him sleep.

MAGDALINA

A huge smile creasing her face:

"Bonjour somnolent."

(Hello sleepy)

ISABELLE

Making her way to the large doors:

"I will go fetch some water."

She stops in mid stride:

"Do you hear that?"

The sound of horses can be heard within the forest.

MICHAEL

"We have to get out of here now."

CAPRON

"I agree."

Capron opens one of the back doors and just as he takes a step outside a flaming arrow pierces his chest. The pointed tip of the shaft bursts out of his back extinguished and covered in gore. Capron stumbles backward, shocked to see the feathered shaft of the arrow protruding from his chest. Magdalina reaches for her brother taking hold of him just as he loses his balance and eases him to the floor. Hysterical, she presses her hand against the wound trying to keep his life's blood from leaving his body.

MAGDALINA

"No!"

Crying holding her brother:

"You are going to be ok. It's not so bad. Get up, please."

CAPRON

Capron looks up at his sister, places his hand on her cheek and smiles as his eyes tear up:

"Vous êtes mon meilleur ami."

(You are my best friend.)

Isabelle and Michael watch helplessly as Capron's hand falls away from his sister's face, then takes his last breath. Magdalina shakes her brother hoping he will wake up, but he doesn't. She looks at Michael, her tears roll down her face washing away the dirt on her cheeks.

MAGDALINA

"No!"

Another burning arrow zips through the window and lands in a pile of dry straw igniting it instantly. The fire spreads through the barn traveling from piles of dried hay to even dryer wood planks until it has engulfed the entire barn. The trio pay the growing fire no mind.

MAGDALINA CONT'D

Crying:

"Please bring him back."

Michael bites his lip as his eyes glass over. He slowly shakes his head and looks down.

MICHAEL

"I can't."

Isabelle looks up at Michael as if her world had just shattered. Her emotions take hold of her.

ISABELLE

"Why not? You are Michael. Can't you do something?"

MICHAEL

"I can't! I'm sorry"

Michael tries to hold back the tears, but he can't. They flow like rivers down his face.

The blaze quickly spreads throughout the little farm house. Support beams grow weak and tumble down to the already blackened wood floor shattering it. Magdalina, Isabelle and Michael take a moment of silence for Capron as the walls are consumed by the flames. When Michael realizes that the main supports for the old house is starting to crack and crumble, he grabs Isabelle and Magdalina and drags them out of the burning house.

EXT. OUT SIDE THE BURNING SHACK- DEEP IN WOODS

They fall to the floor coughing and a man dressed in full black and silver battle armor walks up to Michael. Coughing and gasping for air, Michael tries to get up. The man kicks him in the face with an armored boot. Michael's head bounces off of a rock imbedded in the ground. His vision begins to fade as he struggles to keep his eyes open.

Michael can hear the screams of Magdalina and Isabelle as he slowly loses consciousness. He can see them being dragged away and put on horseback by the men who have accompanied the knight dressed in black. Everything goes dark.

The knight kneels down, then pulls the hood from Michael's head, grabs him by the hair and looks at him as if he were a common peasant. Letting go of Michael's hair, the man rises to his feet, wipes his hands on a handkerchief and gestures for his men to take the unconscious "Angel" away.

JACOB

"Take this trash away."

Two knights step forward, bind Michael's legs and arms then fling his body over the back of a waiting horse. Isabelle screams for Michael to wake up but the only response she gets is an open palm slap across her face from one of the armed men. The knights ride off with their captives in to the woods.
The blackened husk that was once Capron's body rests on the floor of the farm house, just as Magdalina had left him. The skin on his flesh is eaten away by the fire and the bones turned to cinder. The once peaceful farm house in the middle of the woods is completely consumed by the raging inferno.

CHAPTER 11

INT. THE POPE'S CHAMBERS

Inside the Pope's chambers, the servants drag away what is left of the mangled corpse of the woman. Chamber maids kneel on bruised knees, scrubbing relentlessly to get the blood cleaned up from the dark wood floor. The elderly Pope sits in a decorative chair by the large fireplace throwing the woman's severed fingers in the flames and watching them burn one by one.

INT. CASTLE

Jacob returns to the castle with his prizes. The men gathered by the portcullis hoot and holler at the ladies slung over the horses. Pages move in to take the reins of the horses as the knights dismount. Jacob motions for a couple of female servants to take the women and clean them up. Michael begins to stir as he is pulled from the horse. The guards smack him around a bit and then drag him down to the dungeons.

The guards strip Michael of his belongings on the way down. Seeing that some of the guards are trying to make off with the

"Angel's" possessions, Jacob takes the items and hands them off to a trusted page for safe keeping and later inspection. Jacob walks through the lavishly decorated halls, he confidently approaches the Pope's door and request an audience with him. The chamber guards open the door and Jacob walks through.

INT. THE POPE'S CHAMBERS

The morning light from outside shines through the windows and illuminates the large room. The room is quiet and sparse with the Pope sitting in his chair by the fireplace still tossing body parts in the fire. The acrid smell of burning flesh fills the air. Sitting by the fire the old Pope lifts his head when he hears approaching footsteps. Without looking at the man, his eyes are glazed in anticipation of the news.

POPE JOHN XXIII

"Back so soon my son?"

Jacob walks to the Pope, kneels, and kisses his ring.

POPE JOHN XXIII CONT'D

"What news do you bring me?"

JACOB

Looks up at the Pope with excitement:

"He is in the dungeon my Lord. We have prepared him for your visit."

A savage grin stretches across the Pope's wrinkled face as he throws the last finger into the fire. The flesh bubbles up, the finger nail turns black and shrivels in a cloud smoke. The severed finger shrinks as the moisture is being stripped from the flesh. The Pope stares at the fire, pleased by the news.

INT. DARK DUNGEOUN

Michael wakes to a damp dirty cell. His arms have been chained to the wall so long that they are beginning to go numb. The wet stone behind him digs into his back every time he attempts to stand on the tips of his toes to take the pressure off of his shoulders. He notices the chill in the air and that his clothes and equipment are gone. He begins to panic and struggles to free himself.

Light filters through small circular holes near the ceiling on the opposite side of the room, projecting beams of light across the entire length of the dark cell. A small form lies dead on the other side of the room. The blood that stains his body is still runny and fresh. The form of the being looks wrong due to the welts along its arms and body. It takes a moment for Michael to realize that the old man's bones have been completely shattered and threatening to break through the skin. The thinning silver hair on the dead man's head rings bells in Michael's mind. He realizes that the dead man across from him is the same man who was taken away only a few days earlier.

Michael hears a door open. Bright shards of light from beyond the doorway pierce through the darkness and illuminate the particles that drift through the air. The bright light is quickly blotted out as the body of a soldier leads the way from the halls, with two other men following closely behind. They walk down the steps to Michael's cell.

JACOB

"Open it."

The other guard opens the door and steps to the side allowing room for Jacob to walk in.

MICHAEL

"Who the fuck are you?"

Jacob gives Michael a solid left hook to the gut that causes Michael to lose his breath. The blow slams his body against the jagged rocks behind him, tearing his skin and puncturing his back in some places. Michael's head droops as he coughs out the air from his lungs.

JACOB

"You will hold your foul tongue in the presence of your Holiness."

Michael laughs and spits in Jacob's eye. The man, still clad in full armor, calmly wipes the spittle off of his face. He punches Michael in the stomach then he immediately grabs him by the neck and chokes him cutting off his air supply. Michael looks the man in the eyes, robbing him of the satisfaction of watching him suffer.

POPE JOHN XXIII

Just outside the cell door:

"That is enough Jacob."

The Pope enters the tiny cell and Jacob releases Michael then steps away. The small robed man steps between Michael and Jacob.

POPE JOHN XXIII CONT'D

"The people are saying that you are the Arch Angel, Michael. I don't see any heavenly wings on your back. Why is this?"

MICHAEL

Lifts head and chuckles:

"That's because I'm not a fucking bird jack ass."

Jacob moves in to strike Michael, but the Pope calmly raises his hand to stop him.

POPE JOHN XXIII

"You have no wings because you are just a man. A man who I will take great pleasure in breaking and when that is done I will consume your power. Your soul will be mine to devour and savor. First, I have two fresh birds waiting in my chambers. I do believe you know them."

Michael lunges at the depraved man to beat him senseless, but his bonds hold him in place.

"Don't worry I will get to you soon enough."

The wolf in sheep's clothing turns and heads back up the stairs. Jacob punches Michael in the groin. The shackles prevent Michael from doubling over. The arrogant Knight takes hold of Michael's head, slams it into the wall before leaving. A warm sensation trickles down the back of Michael's head. Once the two men reach the top of the steps, another guard enters the cell with a red hot branding iron in the shape of a cross and presses it against the exposed chest of Michael. The skin sizzles at the touch of the super-heated metal. The outside door closes.

EXT. IN THE HALL

The Pope and Jacob walk away from the dungeons. The anguished screams of Michael filter through the thick doors of the dungeon and spill out in to the court yard. The Pope hears him, smiles and walks away.

CHAPTER 12

INT. BATH CHAMBERS

Inside the castle, chamber maids bathe Isabelle and Magdalina in a large tub with gold trim. The two women look around uncomfortably. One of the chamber maids comes through the door with fresh under clothes and dresses, laying them out on a nearby bench.

MAGDALINA

"What is going on?"

The chamber maids look at each other and say nothing. The entire time that the two ladies have been in the presence of the servants, not one of them tried to meet their gaze. They look to the floor or focus harder on whatever task they happen to be doing, but never looking them eye to eye.

MAGDALINA CONT'D

"Qu'est-ce qui se passe?"

(What is going on?)

A fair looking chamber maid pauses for a moment then looks at the others in the large room exchanging a sorrowful glance. The eldest of the chamber maids nods at the young woman and she turns back to the frightened ladies. For a long moment it seemed that the woman was working up the courage to speak to them. Once the woman felt she had the confidence of the other maids around her, she looked at Magdalina, finally meeting her eyes and opens her mouth to expose the stub of a tongue. She uses her hand and runs it up and down the nub to signal to her that it has been cut out.

Magdalina's eyes water and she covers her mouth to keep from screaming as she looks in horror at the mangled flesh that used to be the young woman's tongue. The two ladies move closer to one another. Magdalina holds Isabelle in an attempt to keep her body from trembling.

Jacob barges into the room. The chamber maids drop their heads and frantically get back to work cleaning the ladies.

JACOB

"Hurry and make them worthy to be in the presence of our Holiness."

The chamber maids look at each other with fear in their hearts and comply with the man's orders. Jacob grins at the ladies, turns and exits the room.

INT. DARK DUNGEOUN

The musty smell of wet rock, dirt and feces fill the air inside the dark cell. Michael hangs beaten and battered. His right eye swollen, cheeks cut and blood dripping from his mouth. He looks down to see that flies have already started gathering on his burnt chest and though it hurts to do so, he wiggles his body trying to ward them off. With every second that passes his hope of getting out of this alive dwindles.

The door just beyond the cell opens and a man sneaks down the steps and looks inside the cramped space. The man wears the uniform of a guard, but is smaller than the others Michael had seen thus far. His facial hair is dirty and unkempt, his skin rugged, but not from battle. The man looks like a farmer.

MICHAEL

"I know you're there. I think you guys have met your ass kicking quota for the day."

The figure just beyond the bars crouches down, almost as if he's trying to get a better look at the chained man. Michael notices that he almost turns around and heads back up the stairs, but decides against it. The man hesitates before speaking.

JACQUES

"I've heard the people talk about you. They tell stories of the angel that has come to save us. I see only a man, but I know that God works in mysterious ways to bring about His will."

Michael looks over at the middle aged man with his good eye. The man winces when he sees that Michael's right eye swollen shut. He forces a smile.

MICHAEL

"What is up with you people? Your faith in God amazes me. Well, you are dressed for the part, are you gonna take your share of cheap shots?"

JACQUES

"I would not dream of it. The people believe you are a messenger from God, as do I. I wish to help you. I have found where they keep your possessions and will gladly take you to retrieve them."

MICHAEL

"This door isn't going to unlock itself."

Jacques smiles ruefully and shows Michael that he has a key, then proceeds to open the door. Michael's head perks up as he is filled with adrenaline. He didn't think that someone would actually risk their life to save a complete stranger. After Jacques opens the door, he immediately goes to release Michael from his shackles. Michael's legs are numb and when he tries to stand he falls to the floor.

MICHAEL

"You are risking your life to help me. Why?"

Picking up Michael and looks him in the eyes:

"Because I am a man of God. I know what it means to walk the line between evil and good. I am Jacques, and I think we can help each other."

Jacques slings one of Michael's arms around his shoulders and wraps his arm around the battered man's body to support him. They walk up the steps into a hall that leads away from the tiny cell, making sure to stay as silent as possible so they don't alert the real guards on patrol. With every step Michael can feel his strength returning and begins to support more of his own weight as they make their way to the courtyard.

EXT. COURTYARD

They come to an opening that leads outside into the large courtyard. They press themselves against the wall and check for the guards roaming the grounds. The area seems empty for now and so they continue to move along to an archway that leads into the castle.

INT. CASTLE HALL

The torches do little to illuminate the dark hall. Not even the sinking sun offers enough light to illuminate the passages. Pressed against the wall, Michael checks behind him to make sure they haven't been discovered. Utilizing his military training, Michael pays extra attention to the noises around him making sure to whisper when he needs to communicate with Jacques.

MICHAEL

"How much further?"

JACQUES

"Not much farther now. We will find your belongings in that room there."

Jacques points to a door at the end of the corridor. Just as they begin to move an armored guard carrying a long spear turns down the hall, spots the two of them and charges like a mad bull. Jacques cringes and ducks down while Michael jumps in front of him. With renewed strength, Michael runs at the guard, grabs the spear, and falls back while kicking the guard over him. Michael rolls on top of the guard using every ounce of strength in him to hold down metal clad man. Jacques kicks the helmet and knocks it off the struggling guard's head, then Michael leans back, then forward, repeatedly head butting the guard. Michael doesn't stop until he hears the other man's skull crack. The dutiful guard stops moving. Michael gets up and runs to the door Jacques pointed to earlier, looks around and finds his equipment draped over a chest.

CHAPTER 13

INT. POPE'S CHAMBERS

Isabelle and Magdalina sit in the Pope's chambers dressed like little girls. The dresses are too small and barely cover their breasts and thighs. The man who escorted them to this room ordered them to sit in the ornate chairs near the large dark wooden desk. The girls fidget in their seats nervously awaiting what is to come. The giant door swings open. Their malevolent host, with his hands clasped together in front of him steps through. Jacob remains outside. He proceeds to close and lock the massive door.

The perverse old man's face cracks, as his lips form a crooked grin. He makes his way over to the two scantily clad ladies, stops in front of them and drinks in the sight. The foul man smiles again and pinches Isabelle's cheek.

POPE JOHN XXIII

"You are even more beautiful than I had imagined."

Isabelle pulls away in disgust. The Pope cocks his head then slaps her in the face nearly knocking the small lady out of her chair.

POPE JOHN XXIII CONT'D

Angered:

"You will not disrespect me in my chambers."

Looking at Magdalina in disappointment:

"What example are you setting, just sitting there like a stubborn ass when she treats me this way?"

The crazy old man raises his hand at Magdalina as if to strike her as well. She does not flinch, but stares him in the eyes defiant. Infuriated, Pope John steps in front of her and with surprising speed he wraps both hands around her throat choking her.

ISABELLE

Jumps on his back and screams:

"You monster!"

The Pope loses his balance and falls back on to his desk. Isabelle takes the full force of the impact and falls to the floor holding her head. Magdalina tries to catch her breath.

POPE JOHN XXIII

The Pope rises to his feet and looks at the feisty woman:

"Such anger in you, my child."

He turns his attention back to Magdalina and just as she tries to stand, he jumps on her, knocking her backward in her chair. They both fall to the floor hard. The back of Magdalina's head cracks against the floor, causing stars to explode before her eyes. Desperately she puts her arms in front of her and tries to push the old man off, but he is too heavy. The enraged man grabs a handful of the struggling woman's hair then he yanks her head to the side. She screams as bones in her neck pop. The Pope leans down, then bites at her throat. He rips off her flesh, and starts chewing as she goes in to shock. Gasping for life saving air, Magdalina begins to choke on her own blood.

Pulling herself up off the floor, using the desk for support, Isabelle grabs a stone paper weight and strikes the Pope in the back of the head, knocking him over and revealing her longtime friend beneath him. She sees that Magdalina is on the floor covered in blood, dead and she begins to cry.

ISABELLE

"You are a devil!"

INT. HALL LEADING TO THE POPE'S CHAMBERS

Just beyond the Anti-Pope's chamber doors, Jacob has his ear pressed against the door taking pleasure in the horrible sounds he hears coming from the other side. With a sick sense of pleasure the young knight presses his whole body against the door while rubbing the wood with his ungloved hands.

Michael marches down the hall followed by Jacques, he can see

Jacob standing at the door, caught in some sort of sick fetish and unaware that his end is only paces away. Michael lifts his gun.

INT. POPE'S CHAMBERS

The Pope looks at Isabelle with rage burning behind his dead eyes and staggers to his feet. Isabelle steps backward as she watches the blood drip from his lips and chin down to his fine robes.

POPE JOHN XXIII

Smiling:

"I will enjoy taking your innocence."

The door explodes in a thunderous crash, leaving blood and wood in its aftermath. The Pope jumps in surprise looking the ruins of his beautiful door. Michael kicks open what's left of the splintered wreck. Jacob's headless body falls into the room. Michael rushes through the door ready to kill the sick old man, but stops when he spots Magdalina on the floor in a pool of blood. The rage in Michael reaches its boiling point and he bolts for the monster wearing the skin of a man.

MICHAEL

"You sick fuck!"

The Pope runs to the far corner of the room and thumbs a tile on the wall and a secret door opens. The frightened man rushes through the secret passage. Michael gives chase.

Jacques runs in and notices that Isabelle is knelt down by Magdalina crying. He rushes over and wraps his arms around her, sorry he couldn't get to her sooner.

JACQUES

"We must go. The royal guards will be here soon and we don't want to be here for that. Viens avec moi chérie."

(Come with me darling.)

INT. NARROW HALL

Michael chases the hopelessly pathetic Pope down a narrow hallway leading out into a grand room. The light from the torches are dim and close to burning out. The light dances from wall to wall leaving eerie shadows to play along the windowless room. Michael hears his quarry in a room just down the narrow passage.

INT. DARK ROOM

In an offshoot of the long dark hall, the room sits void of light. The candles on the wall look as if they have been burning for ages and are about to snuff themselves out. On his knees grasping the clothes of the man, the pathetic Pope begs for his help.

POPE JOHN XXIII

"Please my Lord, don't let him kill me."

The man kicks the graveling old fool off his legs, disgusted that it has come to this. The Pope falls to the floor weeping like a child.

MAN

"I warned you of the consequences of failure."

The dark man kneels down and grabs the frightened Pope by the neck and rips out his Adam's apple. Clutching at his throat in a poor attempt to keep his blood from spilling out, the Pope reaches out with his other hand, still looking for help from the shadowy figure. Michael runs up just as the man turns and walks away deeper into the shadows. Michael stops as an odd feeling of déjà vu strikes him. His gut tells him that the man walking away is the same man from the bunker. Michael tries to chase him, but the man fades into the maze of halls that are steeped in darkness. Michael looks around and see's nothing but the dead Pope still bleeding out on the floor.

EXT. COURTYARD

Jacques and Isabelle are surrounded by two dozen armed guards. Each armored knight moves slowly toward the desperate couple, savoring the moment in which they could satisfy their need for battle, and their sick lust. Jacques backs away slowly keeping himself between the blood thirsty men and Isabelle. The armed brutes inch their way to what they think

*will be an easy victory with a little celebration to top off their
hard work at the end.*

*Awkwardly holding a sword, Jacques tries to fend off the
soldiers. He thrusts the tip of the long blade toward the nearest
of the guards.*

JACQUES

"Back! Get back you dogs!"

*A thunderous crash from above pulls the eyes of everyone
upward. The guards look up in startled amazement when they
see Michael coming down at them, his A.X.L. a blaze and gun
drawn. His new black hooded cloak, courtesy of one headless
Jacob, flutters around him like the wings of a big black bird.
Jacques shields Isabelle as stone and glass from the castle rains
down around them.*

*Michael burns off one of his flashes, blinding the guards
just before he lands hard on the ground. Rising to his full
height, Michael burns holes into the guards with his fiery
glare. The guards stand there, bewildered and not knowing if
they should attack. One of the guards throws his weapon to the
ground and backs away as it clatters against the stone of the
courtyard. The others fall to their knees and beg for forgiveness
from the angel that stands before them. Michael knows that he
should kill them, but can't bring himself to do so. The fear of
the repercussions of how it may alter the future is too great.*

MICHAEL

Glancing at Isabelle and Jacques:

"Isabelle, I think you already know Jacques. I think you should go now."

Michael turns his attention back to the guards as Jacques leads Isabelle out of the courtyard. They pass the gates and head for the stables to borrow a horse. If Isabelle had been in a more stable frame of mind she would have wondered how Michael knew the two were married.

INT. STABLES

Inside the stables, Isabelle turns to Jacques, buries her head in his chest and cries hard. He removes his cloak and wraps it around her shoulders. The trauma of losing her friend in such a horrific way was clearly too much for her mind to handle at that moment and she did the only thing she could do, so the tears flowed freely. Jacques holds her close and tight as the realization that he had almost lost the mother of his children this night crashes over him like a tidal wave.

Michael stands at the entrance looking at them both. He doesn't want to break up this intimate moment but he knows that they should get the hell out of dodge. His head hangs low as he contemplates their options. They could go back to the village where they would most likely be targeted and eventually killed or try to make their home somewhere else. With his mind made up, he makes his way to them and places his hand on

Jacques shoulder.

MICHAEL

"Do you have a safe place to go?"

Jacques lifts his head from Isabelle's hair, eyes red rimmed are moist. He smiles weakly then nods. Isabelle tries with little effect to dry her eyes so she can see her rescuer.

JACQUES

"My farm. We can go there."

ISABELLE

Turns to Michael. Her weeping has slowed but the pain of loss in clear in her motions:

"Thank you. Thank you."

Isabelle abruptly leaves Jacques to embrace Michael in a fierce hug and then the tears begin to flow again. The pressure of the embrace against Michael's chest peels his burnt skin apart and sends needles of pain through his body, but he bites down hard to quell the pain. He hugs her back and for a moment he thought he could actually feel her emotions pouring through him.

MICHAEL

"I'm sorry I could not help Magdalina."

Isabelle shakes her head letting him know that there was probably nothing he could have done differently to save her.

She's just glad that he was there to offer the help they desperately needed.

MICHAEL CONT'D

"I finally know who you two are."

Isabelle looks at Michael confused, then she blinks her eyes rapidly to clear the tears. Using a piece of cloth, Jacques handed her to try and dampen the stream of tears flowing from her eyes, she looks at him curiously. Michael steps closer to them with a genuinely sorrowfully happy smile.

MICHAEL CONT'D

"You two will have a daughter. She will end the war and no matter what happens after she does this, remember, she will become a saint. Now go live your lives and be happy."

Michael turns and walks away. The dazed couple watches him limp away. Worry and hopeful optimism fills their hearts.

JACQUES

"Where will you go?"

Michael turns around and shrugs his shoulders. Michael punches in a date, looks at the couple, waves and disappears.

CHAPTER 14

EXT. MAJESTIC WOODS-SCOTLAND

The dense forest is moist with the flowing mist that carpets the ground like the ancient tendrils of an incorporeal creature. The grey sky above only adds majesty to the mystical forest. Beams of sunlight break through the canopy and reflect off the floating droplets of water. Chilled dew drips from the vines, that cling to the ancient trees down to the densely pack vegetation below like a gentle rain shower.

Una walks through the forest collecting herbs and other plants for her father, and places them in one of the compartments in the leather pouch that hangs from her waist. Her red hair is finally growing back in. She had shaved it in protest so she wouldn't be married off to a man she did not love. Her father had jokingly made remarks about her head looking like an egg and now he cracks jokes about how she looks like a damned pixie.

The loose sleeves of her tunic sway as she moves through the brush. She uses leather straps and colorful cloths to secure the ill-fitting shirt tightly around her body. The dirt and grass stains speak of long hard use and serve as a form of mottled camouflage, breaking up her female form.

Her leather pants are adorned with straps, beads, and many pockets. The stone and steel knives hang in their sheaths, slapping against her thighs with every step. The stone bead belt around her waist flickers in the soft morning light. The tiny bits of shiny stone, serve to shield her from other worldly forces. As with her enchanted jewelry, the knives tucked into her boots are engraved with bindings in the form of intricate knot work from tip to handle. Her long boots tie from the ankle to just below the knee offering a great deal of support when she has to move fast.

She spots something dark far in the distance that does not belong to her forest. She crouches, pulls out one of her stone knives, which had been strapped to her leg, and moves slowly over to the dark form. As she draws closer to the thing, she realizes that it is a man. He is dressed in clothes and materials she has never seen until now. The strange looking man lays unconscious, sprawled over a downed tree. It seemed to her that he had fallen hard and violently knocked his head. She looks at him curiously. His odd style of dress marks him as one who does not belong in her homeland or her world for that matter. He is not a familiar. She doesn't know if this man is friend or foe.

The thought of killing him crosses her mind and she has to fight the urge to end the life of this strange man. She holsters her knife and begins to examine him closer. When she probes his body, she can see that he is badly injured and in need of some serious attention or the minor wounds will fester and kill him.

The glint of metal catches her eye and she examines the odd device that is wrapped around his forearm. Her index finger slides across one of the display screens and the device comes to life. The strange lights startle her at first but the shock of all the colors is quickly replaced by intrigue. She looks him over again finding his weapons and stashes them in her pouch. She puts her hands under Michael's shoulders and begins to drag him away.

INT. INSIDE THE CAVE OF LAILOKEN

Michael slowly opens his eyes and finds that he is in a fire lit cave. Surprisingly the cave is very well kept and made to look very much like a home. Hand paintings of outlandish scenes decorate the walls as well as animal furs and hand crafted steel weapons. Michael knew that who ever lived here had some style. He can feel the cool moss under him as he slowly tests the limits of his battered body. His wounds are cleaned, dressed and he is a little shocked when he discovers that he is not. Save for the fur blanket Michael, is completely in the buff.

Una sits on a rock pressed up against the wall, her head bobbing up and down as she fights off the insistent urge to sleep. She had been sitting there waiting for the strange man from the forest to wake up for three days. Michael can see another room, also lit by fire just beyond the young lady's perch. Strange shadows dance along the walls and Michael can *tell that someone seems to be working in there.*

Una notices that Michael is awake and pops off of the rock like a coiled spring beneath her had been released. Once back on solid ground the girl crawls up to him with a giant childlike smile. Her amber eyes are entrancing and Michael finds it hard to look away.

Before either of them could speak there is an explosion in the other room that demands both of their attention but only Michael looks in surprise.

A thin, bearded man with a large dark green cloth wrapped around his body staggers out of the room coughing. His body smokes and his face is covered in yellowish ash. His salt and pepper beard hangs off of his face like a bad shag carpet. Elaborate blue knot work tattoos crisscross his body like a shield of ink.

He's laughing as he fans the smoke away from his face. He stops laughing when he notices Michael sitting up. The older man stiffens and stares at Michael with an odd curiosity flooding his mind with questions. The man drops to all fours, crawls over to Michael and smells him like a dog.

LAILOKEN

"An bhfuil tú rollta timpeall i caca?"

(Have you been rolling around in shit?)

Una laughs at her father's comment but quickly stifles her amusement trying to be the serious one in this encounter with the outsider. She crosses her arms as she tries to be stern but a smile creeps its way back onto her face.

MICHAEL

"What?"

Michael sniffs himself:

"Oh yeah, that."

Moving to stand beside her crouched father, Una looks at Michael trying figure out his origins. She looks him up then down slowly studying every scar and wound. She knows that not even the Roman politicians have the quality materials this man had in his possession.

UNA

"Nuair a tháinig as duit?"

(Where did you come from?)

MICHAEL

"I don't understand what you are saying?"

The father and daughter look at each other in confusion. They both are capable of understanding many languages and it bothers them that they do not understand a word the naked man has spoken.

LAILOKEN

"Ní thuigim cad tá á rá aige."

(I don't understand what he is saying)

Una points at Michael and lifts her hands to her sides, to indicate that they don't understand his words. Understanding flows over Michael and he thinks of a way he could communicate with his hosts. Michael looks at the young lady and points to his armband that rests close to his clothes on a hand carved wooden table. Following his gesture, Una spots what he is pointing to and cautiously moves to gather his things. Once the items are in her hands she examines them, but not as intensely as she had over the past three days. This time she knows she will get answers to the questions that have been plaguing her mind. Making sure to keep a wary eye on the man she hands over his possessions.

Michael practically drops everything else and looks at the date on the T.D.B. It reads Glasgow, Scotland July 19, 521.

Michael shows them the year and date. The father and daughter nod in understanding, then Michael twists the dial up to the year of 2113.

The father and daughter look at each other in disbelief. Una just stares at the date, then at Michael in pure amazement and a bit of satisfaction as most of her questions are answered. While his daughter looks at the man completely captivated, Lailoken stands trying to process what the young man is showing him then looks back at Michael dumbfounded.

Michael points to the other room where Lailoken was working and expresses interest. The old man gestures for Michael to follow as he walks over to the next room.

Michael pulls on his pants, then with help from Una, he slowly *and painfully pulls himself up and follows the old man in to the other room.*

INT. THE SPELL ROOM-CAVE

Lailoken puts his hand over a small bowl of yellow powder and with nothing more than a thought, the bearded man ignites it. Then he uses his energy to make the flames rise to his hands and transport it to a pot filled with a thick liquid. The liquid burst into blue flames then quickly snuffs out. Amazement and absolute disbelief cripples Michael's brain. He can't believe that he just may be in the presence of a real life wizard. Many thoughts and questions rush through his head. Michael asks for their names.

The old wizard looks at him puzzled then Michael points to himself trying to establish some sort of first name familiarity with the two of them.

MICHAEL

"Mi-ch-ael Art-urius Cor-tez."

Then he points to Lailoken and Una. The older man looks at him strangely but understanding is clear in the young lady's eyes. She claps wildly and smiles.

UNA

Puts her hand to her chest:

"Oo-n-ah Guinevar"

Nodding his head as if saying, "I get it now" and feeling a bit slow in the head the old wizard points to himself.

LAILOKEN

"La-lo-icen."

A few days pass as Michael takes some time to heal from the injuries he sustained in France. Finally being able to move more freely than when he had first arrived, Michael limps into the work room where Lailoken toils with some powders, herbs and liquids. Una sits on a wooden chair by some shelving, cataloging every item stacked on the knotted wood by torch light. She pauses when Michael steps into the room.

Michael smiles and points to the bowl of fire to as if ask if Lailoken could show him how he had created the amazing demonstration a few days earlier. Lailoken bops Michael on the forehead. Confused, Michael looks to Una who is sitting perched on the chair giggling.

Una laughs and points to her head to indicate to Michael that it's all in the mind. Lailoken takes Michael by the hand, faces it palm down over the black powder. The graying man signals for Michael to breath and focus by taking a few deep breaths himself. Nodding his head, Michael complies with the unspoken request. Breathing deeply Michael envisions a flame in his mind's eye that grows to a raging inferno and for a few moments nothing happens. Doubt creeps into his mind but he quickly pushes it out. Concentrating harder, he focuses on the immense heat that the fire in his mind would produce if he were right in front of it. Michael can feel the energy traveling through his body. Beads of sweat roll down his face.

Lailoken feels the immense energy flowing from the man and looks to his daughter to make sure that he's just not imagining it. She nods. Michael feels his skin radiating heat and abruptly an image of his mother flickers through his thoughts. Before Michael can shut it out the emotions tied to the thought ignites a surge of energy and he produces a spark. In complete shock, Michael opens his eyes to see the bowl burning with a gentle flame dancing at its center. The old Mage's jaw drops in amazement at what the young man was able to achieve and in the span of a millisecond. Michael jumps for joy. Una laughs as she rocks in her chair applauding, Michael's success. The wizard, however, looks on the spectacle entangled in deep but appreciative thought. He had never seen a person let alone a grown man utilize the innate force of the talent so quickly. The flow of energy that emanated from the distant traveler was something the old mage had never seen in a human.

UNA

Laughing at Michael:

"'s sé agus corr amháin."

(He's an odd one.)

Una and Michael smile at each other as the aging wizard slaps Michael on the back in congratulations. The unsure crease of a smile creeps onto the old man's face. The implications of this man's arrival and his gargantuan talent trouble the old wizard.

CHAPTER 15

Months have passed since Michael first appeared in the forest. With that passing of time the seasons had naturally changed, bringing the chill of winter and though, the grass is still green the wind bites at the flesh and the freezing rains penetrates down to the marrow of the bone. The big game still runs, the Shepherd's still tend to their flocks. Every once in a great while, the Horse Lords roam through the land with trade and tall tales from beyond the Isles which gather many folks who want to hear their stories. The children always run up to meet them as they ride into the village.

Michael has been working closely with the wizard and his daughter, learning all that he can and they are overjoyed to teach him, now that the awkwardness has somewhat passed. His stumbles are few, but his successes are many. He feels that he is starting to feel like he has an actual home to call his own. The simplicity of this new life has given him new hope, which washes out the worries and troubles of his past.

EXT. DIRT ROAD

The trip to the village's market is always something that young Una had always enjoyed. The children playing all around her is her favorite part of it. There is one boy in particular that always tries to steal what medicines she brings to barter with. He hasn't been successful, but they both consider it a mutual challenge to get one over on the other.

Upon Una's return trip home from the village marketplace stocked with food and supplies for the coming winter she whistles while she walks. The large wood and hide rucksack on her back is practically bursting at the seams with goods her and her father can't find in the forest. She kicks the tiny stones lying on the Roman road, watching them skip and bounce ahead of her while thinking about the strange outlander at her home. She had never felt anything for a man. In fact, she had always thought of them as single minded brutes, with her father being an exception. However, Michael has piqued her curiosity and she wants to ask him to stay, but doesn't want him to get the wrong impression. Her thoughts are cut short when she looks at the sky and spots the incoming storm. The clouds in the sky threaten rain but it seems a long way off, besides she can't smell the moisture, yet.

Further on down the road she notices the ambush that lies several meters ahead. The men have done such a piss poor job at concealing themselves in the surrounding brush that even a blind man would not have missed them. The bright red dye of their clothes practically screams from beyond the green and brown shrubs. She has to squash the urge to stop, point and laugh hysterically at the bumbling idiots. Thinking on her feet she affects the persona of a young innocent girl full of the naiveté that goes hand and hand with youth. When she is "ambushed" by the pack of Roman thieves with makeshift weapons drawn, she had grown bored with the act and not having the time or the patience, her shoulders sag in annoyance.

The first man standing in front of her wore a bucket helmet that was too big for his narrow head and he had to keep adjusting it to keep the thing from falling into his eyes every time he moved. The cloaks they wore had a layer of dirt baked into the fabric. All the men were dressed the same and had scars on their wrist and ankles from years spent chained in metal fetters. Una looks at the four men, tired annoyance plain in her face.

BUCKETHEAD THIEF

"Look at what we have here... such a pretty little thing all by herself."

PERVERT THIEF

"She looks like she has a nice tight pocket for my little man. What do you say lads? Should we show her a good time?"

The four men chuckle to each other and begin to circle Una. She looks around at the men smiling inwardly then, rolls her shoulders so that her bag slides off and down to the ground. She charges the thief in front of her, and slams her palm upward into the man's nose killing him instantly. The man crumbles to the ground in a heap. Una turns to face the others with her knife drawn and ready to castrate the first idiot who tries to whip out his, "little man".

JOLLY GIANT THIEF

"You bitch!"

The men charge Una with weapons swinging, but Una uses an energy push to throw the nearest of them back into the others knocking them over. She runs to get some distance between her and her aggressors. The remaining bandits climb to their feet and give chase.

Una runs up a tree, pushing off the trunk at the apex performing a full layout, burying her knife up to the hilt in the neck of the giant would be criminal. The momentum of her controlled fall drags him to the ground with such force his head cracks when it slams into one of the large roots. The big man's body spasms as the trauma to his head had set off some fireworks in his brain. Foamy crimson bubbles seep from his mouth and in rivulets stream down his cheek into the dirt, collecting in a pool.

The last two men back away slowly. Their weapons half drawn and it's obvious from the look on their faces that they do not know how to continue the attack on the small deadly woman. Bucket head tries to take a few steps back, but his rapist buddy nudges him forward. The two men can't make up their minds on how to proceed, so Una makes the choice for them.

Una runs at them, leaping feet first on Buckethead, her stone knife digging deep in to the man's chest tearing flesh and muscle. With her feet planted firmly on either side of his chest, she rides him down crushing the small man's ribcage and shattering his breast plate. Una straightens her legs then leaps off of the broken man and onto the perverted one. Her legs wrapping around his neck, she drops backward causing the man to flip over her driving his head into the ground breaking his neck in a wet crunch.

Una stands up and begins to search the sashes and purses of the dead men. She finds a few gold and silver coins. She tucks them in her pouch, collects their weapons and attaches them to her belt. She'll use them as fuel for the fire tonight to keep her stew hot.

Una leisurely walks back over to her supplies to collect them. She hoists the giant bag onto her shoulders while she begins to whistle an old tune and continues to walk back home with a new bounce in her step.

INT. LAILOKEN'S CAVE

Una returns home to find her father dancing naked in the spell room. She arrives just in time to see the old man shaking his cheeks to a rhythm only he could hear. Horrified she covers her eyes, drops the supplies, and then turns around to face a wall. She desperately tries to purge the liver spotted image from her mind with no luck. The image is forever burned into her mind and her eyes water at the thought of her father's spotted tattooed ass shaking. She hopes this moment will not be the one thing she remembers when she dies.

UNA

"Ní fhaca mé gá chun do thóin wrinkled seanfhear."

(I did not need to see your wrinkled ass old man.)

Surprise hits the old mage like a punch in the stones then he turns around covering his manhood. With eyes as wide as saucers he experiences several emotions at once, and then he just laughs. He knows that he has probably scarred her for life. Lailoken retrieves his tartan from a small stone table and begins wrapping it around his body. After drying the tears of his mirth, he chuckles while trying to catch his breath.

LAILOKEN

"Ó tá brón orainn, ceann óg."

(Oh sorry, young one.)

Still facing the opposite wall and with annoyance tainting her voice, Una examines one of the more elaborate and darker paintings her father had done.

UNA

"I gcás ina ndéanfar Michael?"

(Where is Michael?)

Her father walks out of the room. Synching his leather belt around his waist to secure his clothes. Lailoken stops a couple of paces behind her, then responds to her question by pointing to another painting of a landscape that looks out to the sea. Una ties her cloak tighter around her body, waves at her father without looking back and heads out of the cozy dwelling.

EXT. MOUNTAIN CLIFFSIDE

Michael stands on the edge of the cliff side looking out to the growing clouds and restless sea. Sporting a new thicker wool cloak, the chill air blowing in from the ocean barely touches his skin. He takes a deep breath and smiles. The waves crash against the rocky beach. The salty mist of the ocean floats on the winds. Michael breathes it all in and exhales the strife that has plagued his mind since the start of his adventure.

Una makes her way out of the copse of trees. Once she cleared the thickets, she spots the black clad man easily against the steel blue sky. Trying not to smile she walks the small distance over to where Michael stands. A gust of wind catches her unaware and nearly blows her cloak and hood open, but she pulls the furs and wool closer to her body.

UNA

"An maith leat é anseo?"

(Do you like it here?)

Michael jumps, startled, and turns around to find Una standing behind him enjoying the beautiful vista dressed and bound in wool and furs similar to his own. The dark colors of her winter apparel accentuate the flowing strands of scarlet hair under her hood. Her milky skin and her golden eyes practically glow in the natural light.

MICHAEL

"It's peaceful here."

Una looks at him and smiles. She still can't understand his language, but she can see the tranquility in his eyes. The trouble that was once there is fading by degrees with each passing day.

MICHAEL CONT'D

"You don't know what I'm saying do you?"

Leaning toward him she pats his back three times and smiles warmly at him. She knows that he is taking this time to reflect on whatever has been eating away at him. She can't imagine what had happened to him before he had arrived in her forest.

UNA

"is féidir liom a rá leat é anseo."

(I can tell you like it here.)

Not wanting to take up any more of his time, Una turns and walks away, leaving Michael to his thoughts. She has to check on the stew she had prepared early that morning. Michael watches the nubile woman head toward the forest of the hidden cave then turns back to the ocean for one last glance before following Una back home.

CHAPTER 16

The winter's frost fades from the land revealing the emerald vegetation under the crystalline blanket. Many small animals wake and stir with activity as the warmth of the sun breathes new life into the land. The new generation of hares scurry through the meadows while larger animals graze on the grass. A cool breeze dances through the bushes singing its song of gentle caress as it leisurely flows through the Isle.

EXT. ROCKY BEACH-GIANTS CAUSEWAY

Lailoken tutors Michael in the ways of mage craft. The progress is slow coming, but at a steady pace of improvement. Michael has learned how to use his life force to push objects a small distance. To show the potential of such feats, Lailoken leads his new apprentice to a beach and shows him scattered rocks partially raised out of the water. The old wizard raises his hands and the rocks begin to shutter and grow in height as they rise forming giant pillars on the beach. More stone pillars rise out of the water forming a larger wall behind the first set of stones. *The process continues for several moments until there are multiple layers of stone columns that vary in height and thickness.*

MICHAEL

Looks on in wonder:

"Aww. I wanna do shit like that."

Una sits on a rock and laughs at Michael's behavior as she watches him jump up and down like an excited child.

INT. LAILOKEN'S CAVE-MIDDLE OF THE NIGHT

Beyond the cave the vegetation gleams with the silver kiss of the moon's light breaking through the forest canopy. Nocturnal insects sing their songs. The fires in the cave have burned down to glowing embers. Michael lies on a straw mat on the ground inside the spell room awake. Thoughts of his former life seem insignificant now that he feels that he has found a home.

Michael hears someone creeping inside the cave and heading into the spell room. He thought his roommates were asleep in the other chambers. Michael props himself on his elbows alert at the unexpected intrusion. He begins to sit up ready to pounce when Una pokes her head around the wall. Her body is just a silhouette against the effulgence of the night, but her vermillion hair radiates like a beacon.

Una waves at Michael to follow her into the summer night.

Michael gets up and walks over to where Una stands pressed against the wall. She looks at him smiling and presses a finger to his lips cutting him off from saying a word before he has had a chance to part his lips.

UNA

"Tá áthas orm go bhfuil tú suas. Ba mhaith liom rud éigin a thaispeáint duit."

(I'm glad you are up. I want to show you something.)

Michael looks at her and shakes his head to signify that he does not understand what she had said to him. Rolling her eyes at the small problem, Una grabs Michael by his shirt, drags him outside, through the trees and up the mountain.

EXT. MOUNTAIN SIDE-CLEAR NIGHT

Una leads Michael out of the forest to another clearing on the mountain side. She leads him up to the edge of the cliff side and sits down in the grass looking up at the sky with the most beautifully wide smile Michael had ever seen.

Following her gaze, Michael stands in awe of the meteor shower taking place in the Heavens. Una shifts her eyes to Michael, grabs his hand, and pulls him to the ground to watch the shower of light with her. The two lay on their backs watching the glowing space rocks rain down and burn away in the atmosphere. The streaks of fiery light hurdle through the sky by the hundreds. The fireworks of man pale in comparison to the majesty of nature's magnificent light show.

UNA

Turns and looks at Michael:

"Nach álainn seo?"

(Isn't this beautiful?)

Michael had never seen the sky in such a way before. The many cities he had spent time in as a youth, were so bright that the only light that can be seen during the night was the dimly light moon that was so far away and seemed so small. Here the trillions and trillions of stars shines as bright as the giant moon. No smog or pollution blotting out the skies and poisoning the air. Everything is just so clean and Michael feels that he is seeing the world for the very first time.

Michael knows that Una feels something for him and he for her. The quick stolen glances his way have not gone unnoticed and he's pretty sure that she has noticed him doing the same. So far communication has been limited to gestures or meaningful looks and they have now become very adept at reading each other's body language. Right now, the nonverbal language of their bodies were reaching out to one another with a loud vibrant passion. Feeling wanting eyes on him, Michael turns his head to look at Una.

MICHAEL

"Just my luck, I finally meet a hot girl who's actually interested in me and I can't understand a damn thing she's saying."

Michael smiles at Una, and she smiles back.

The two of them lay there star struck as the orange yellow balls streak across the sky.

EXT. LAILOKEN'S CAVE-ENTRANCE

Michael and Una sit by a fire to ward off the autumn chill as he shows her the T.D.B. and the flash burner.

Una presses a button on the magnesium burner and blinds Michael. She laughs when his hand swings up and smacks across his eyes to shield them from further assault. In his flailing, Michael couldn't hear Una rising to the balls of her feet from her seated position. She pounces on him. They roll along the ground snapping twigs, crunching over dried leaves and very nearly rolling into the small fire before they come to a stop. Michael's eyes focus again to see Una, lying on top of him breathing heavily and smiling. The twigs and leaves sprouting from her hair like the antlers of a deer makes her look like a true lady of the Fae.

They look at one another for a long moment, burning this image, this playful memory into their mind's eye for safe keeping. Lailoken looks on from inside the cave taking a few puffs from the smoldering herbs in his pipe, smiles, and walks inside to give them some privacy. The old magician is happy that his daughter has finally found a man she is comfortable enough to share her feelings with. He knew that the connection between them was there even before they had.

Michael lifts his head up a bit as Una slowly lets hers drift downward. They share their first kiss on a cool autumn night.

INT. LAILOKEN'S CAVE-SPELL ROOM

The flowers and other plant life begin to bloom outside. Michael sits cross legged at the mouth of the cave mixing concoctions in a clay bowl. Lailoken begins to cough a bit to cover his amused chuckling. He removes the pipe from his mouth and gives Michael some more herbs, powders and liquids to mix. Michael mixes a concoction that seems to do nothing. The knowing smile fades from the old wizards face and they both peer inside the mixing bowl. It explodes. Lailoken and Michael enter the main room of the homely cave covered in black ash laughing uncontrollably due to the gas.

INT. LAILOKEN'S CAVE-MAIN ROOM

The icy rain pelts the Earth. The thunder outside rumbles through the sky while the young couple sits near the opening of the cave teaching each other their native tongues. The fire dances and licks the bottom of a pot lending its heat to the meal of the day. Una smiles at Michael, happy that she is finally going to be able to hold a conversation with the man she's fallen in love with, that doesn't involve hand signs, gestures or odd looks. Michael meets her eyes, smiles and in her native language he speaks slowly, unsure that he was saying what he thought properly. He wasn't sure if he was butchering her native tongue.

UNA

Speaking broken English:

"I-Has-Red-Hairs. You-Has-Cute."

MICHAEL

"Tá-tú-álainn..."

(You are beautiful.)

They both pause and look deeply into each other's eyes. They move in close to one another and their lips meet.

EXT. OUTSIDE LAILOKEN'S CAVE

Michael uses his A.X.L. to weld his father's gun to the magnesium flash burner to make it one complete unit. Lailoken sits by the entrance of the cave smoking the weeds in his pipe and Una lays on a branch in a tree pulling leaves from a nearby low hanging limb and letting them drift to the earth. Michael attaches the modified gauntlet to his arm and tests it out.

He sets off a flash, then lowers his hand and presses the trigger to fire off a shot. The thunderous boom startles the father, daughter and any other creature that may have been in the area.

Una falls out of the tree and like a cat she lands on her feet holding her ears. Michael nods with a satisfied smile.

CHAPTER 17

EXT. MEADOW

Una and Michael lay on an island of stone in a meadow that is home to a small but peaceful pond.

The grassland surrounding the body of water is periodically kissed by the subtle eddy of the lazy waves. High in the sky the sun offers its heat to the rocks and in turn the rocks share that heat with the two lovers that lay atop them.

The young couple had been exchanging stories of their life for most of the morning. Una lays next to Michael resting her head on his chest, tracing her finger over the cross shaped scar. Michael shares with Una his journey through time and how he had come to be here in the Isles. Una cried when she had learned the fate of a woman who had yet to be born. It was odd for her. On one hand, these events had not yet taken place, wouldn't take place for hundreds of years and on the other, they already had and were ancient history according to the man telling the story. She didn't know exactly how such things were possible, though she had heard tales from her father about other worlds and creatures from these worlds periodically finding their way to realm of man, so the possibility of such things were not completely lost on her.

UNA

Looking at Michael:

"What was life like where you came from?"

MICHAEL

Eyes closed thinking of the right words:

"It was complicated. Dirty. We had the illusion of freedom, while being bound to thoughtless consumption. The people with the power wanted a docile workforce so they could pay them next to nothing while they lived lavishly. Spirituality along with religion had been banned. If you were caught practicing either it was punishable by death. It was nothing like here and now. Everything is clean and fresh."

Michael dips his chin onto his chest to look at the golden eyes of the woman he loves. He can see the curiosity in her eyes and she can see the new and alien but welcomed peace in his.

MICHAEL CONT'D

"I love it here."

Una smiles lifting herself up off the rock and grabs Michael's hand. She leads him down off their perch and kisses him. Playfully Una runs down to where land meets the water, strips off her top and looks back at Michael laughing.

UNA

"You are dirty and you need to be cleansed. Come to me so I may clean you."

She signals Michael to join her as she takes off the rest of her clothes and runs into the water.

Michael takes off his clothes and meets Una in the slightly chilled water. They drift into the center of the almost still waters, never taking their eyes away from one another.

UNA CONT'D

"You make me so happy. Promise me you will stay."

MICHAEL

Drifting closer to Una:

"I love you more than words can say."

They kiss as they slowly swirl in the center of the pond. Michael pulls away slowly, resting his head on hers. Their eyes are closed, savoring the moment. Tasting each other's lips, smelling each other, and filing away the memory for later enjoyment. A bird squalls in the trees.

MICHAEL CONT'D

"I will never leave you."

They kiss again passionately and begin to make love.

EXT. SMALL VILLAGE

The warm weather of the summer months fades to make way for the cycle of seasons. The farmers harvest the land and prepare for the harvest festival and Samhain, then they'll settle in for the long winter. The children run and play in the village. An old man pulls some produce from what he had harvested off of his wagon and hands it to a new mother caring for her child.

A dog begins to bark wildly in the distance. A large crow caws frantically in one of the large trees. A cold gust of wind rustles through the leaves of the surrounding trees, sending a wicked howling chill through the village that snuffs out most of the fires.

INT. SMALL VILLAGE-TINY HUT

Lailoken sits in a hut talking with the elder of the village. The withered man sitting cross legged never seems to open his eyes. Almost as if he lacks the strength. The silver haired man has been around many years, almost as long as Lailoken. The two old friends discuss old exploits, past rivalries and current developments. The small hearth provides warmth while the pot suspended above the flame boils some meat and potatoes. The smell of the meal fills the small hut and mingles with the aromas of the burning herbs in Lailoken's pipe.

VILLAGE ELDER

Smiling and nodding his head:

"Dá bhrí sin tá an buachaill láidir agus foghlaimíonn sé

go tapa. An-mhaith."

(So the boy is strong and he learns fast. Very good.)

Lailoken pauses for a moment and takes a hit from his pipe. He can't tell if his old friend is being sarcastic or genuinely happy about his stories of the outlander.

LAILOKEN

Smoking a pipe:

"Tá a fhios agam ..."

(I know.)

VILLAGE ELDER

"An bhfuil tú cinnte go bhfuil sé an ceann an tuar Labhair?"

(Are you sure he is the one the prophecy spoke of?)

Lailoken begins to nod his head, because they were finally getting to the meat of the entire conversation. He wanted and needed an outside opinion on this matter. Before the wild mage could speak there is a thunderous boom outside punctuated by the terrified screams of the villagers. Lailoken and the old man rise with speed no one would ever think they possess and exit the small hut. Taking a moment to assess the chaos through the people running for their lives around them they find the cause of all the terror. The lone man they see walking toward them steals the air from their lungs and sends jolting cold chills down their spines, freezing them for only a second, but hesitation can and would be fatal right now.

EXT. SMALL VILLAGE- OUTSIDE

Lailoken never noticed the pipe fall from his lips as he identified the horror before them. The unspeakable terror from ages past strolls through the tiny village killing innocent people indiscriminately. Not even the children are safe from this monster's wrath. Lailoken and his elderly friend never thought that they'd live long enough to see the visage of death walk the Earth again, yet here he was after two thousand years.

Regret hits the two men like a stiff kick to the family jewels. Regret that they had stopped making life extending potions and now they were too old to stop the other worldly demon. The elderly man quivers for the briefest of moments and then disappears, leaving the old mage alone to face the demon. Lailoken had not realized that the old man had left him alone, but judging from past adventures he knew that he would be left to fend for himself like always. Once the aura of the elder couldn't be felt the mage smirks and sucks his teeth in disappointment.

LAILOKEN

Angered:

"Ní raibh mé a rá fhéadfá teacht amach as do pholl!"

(I didn't say you could come out of your hole!)

The murderous demon in human skin tears his attention away from the destruction of the village and directs his hateful glare at Lailoken. For a moment they lock eyes, measuring each other and before the old mage even registers the movement the demon lets loose a tremendous fire ball. Lailoken realizes he cannot move fast enough to deflect the blast. The old wizard makes a cutting gesture behind him and a hole in reality opens to teleport him to the safety of his home. He is a little too slow and the ball travels with him, blasting him out the other side of his rift.

CHAPTER 18

EXT. SHORE FRONT- BEACH AREA

The sun's setting rays reflect in hues of purple and orange against the atmosphere. The waves gently roll against the rocky shore. Michael stands on the beach facing the water. His eyes are closed and his right hand rest at his chest. Most of the rocks on the beach are floating all around him in their own orbits.

An explosion in the mountain shatters his concentration. Michael turns his head to find the source. The rocks drop. Michael rushes towards the cave with fear gripping his heart. He knows that the old man's experiments sometimes explode, but what he had just heard sounded as if two sky cars smashed full speed into each other.

EXT. OUTSIDE LAILOKEN'S CAVE

Michael finds Lailoken injured at the entrance of the cave. His skin is pocked and scorched in places. A pregnant Una is already out of the cave tending to her father, dressing his wounds and asking him what could have done this to him. The complete horror in her eyes tells Michael that this was no potion gone wrong.

MICHAEL

Nervously:

"What happened?"

UNA

Holding her father:

"Cad a tharla athair?"

(What happened father?)

Michael helps Una take her father inside the cave. They make sure not to touch the burns that cover the old mages arms as they carry him.

LAILOKEN

"Tá an ceann dorcha teacht ar ais."

(The dark one has come back.)

INT. LAILOKEN'S CAVE

They lay Lailoken on a bed made of fresh grass. Michael rushes in to the spell room to grab some ointments. When he darts back to the main chamber he begins applying the mixtures to the old man's burns and wounds. Michael hadn't noticed when he initially returned, that Una had stopped moving. She was staring off into space slack jawed and eyes moist. He had never seen any of them in this state and it was starting to freak him the hell out. After many heart beats, Una manages to regain some control.

UNA

"He says the dark one is back."

MICHAEL

"Who is the dark one?"

Lailoken closes his eyes to fall into a much needed healing trance. Una uses this opportunity to take Michael into another room to explain what she knew of the dark one. Michael looks back at the old man who appears to be okay, if you don't count the spots of melted skin.

INT. LAILOKEN'S CAVE-SPELL ROOM

Una sits on a rock as Michael kneels before her. She takes a moment to compose her thoughts so that they come out as her mind intends them.

UNA

"The dark one is an ancient enemy. When I was a small girl my father told me stories about a dark elf that was not of this world. He wanted my father to use his power to open a gateway to the Dark world to release his brethren here in ours. The elf promised everything he could to my father if he did this. My father had time to observe the demon and realized that the dark elf was evil and had no intention of fulfilling any promises nor did the demon want to live peaceably with man. When my father refused, the elf was angered and tried to kill him. For years they fought. Lead by father, the armies of man fought against impossible foes and creatures and one day father found a way to seal the elf away in a jewel."

The history lesson is cut short when a shadow crosses the light and the couple look up to see Lailoken standing at the entrance of the room. His skin looks a little waxy but better than before.

LAILOKEN

Exhausted he speaks with labored breath:

"Tá an ceann dorcha scriosta sráidbhaile ar an taobh thoir ..."

(The dark one has destroyed a village to the east...)

Legs weary and ready to give way, Lailoken is on the verge of collapse. Michael moves to Lailoken to support him, catching the injured man before he falls to the ground. Parts of the old man's tartan flake off and crumble.

LAILOKEN CONT'D

"Ní féidir liom stop a chur air."

(I can't stop him.)

Michael looks at Una with deep concern. The paintings on the walls finally make sense. He had always thought that they were just the works of a wild imagination and not an actual account of history.

UNA

"I don't think that father can stop him this time either."

INT. LAILOKEN'S CAVE-MAIN ROOM

Michael takes the injured old man to his chambers and lays him down on the grass bed. Lailoken looks at Michael intently and with purpose. The mage grabs Michael by his cloak and pulls him close then whispers to him. At first Michael couldn't make out what the old wizard was saying and then it clicked.

LAILOKEN

"You are the one I saw in a dream."

Michael looks at him as the last sequences of the painting are puzzled together. Not only was it a telling of history, it also told of a prophecy about a man that would come and defeat the demon, by biting off parts of his body. Some of the details were still lost on Michael, but it made enough sense.

LAILOKEN CONT'D

"You are the one to stop him."

Michael leans back in shock processing every detail that is running through his mind. Una stands paces away from the entrance of the main room looking at the father of her unborn child and holds her belly as the tears flow from her eyes. Michael stands up, turns, then walks to Una and holds her.

EXT. BURNING VILLAGE

The bloody hand of a woman lies lifeless on the ground, a portion of her head is missing, her other arm still clutches her young wailing child.

The man walks through the village making sure that every structure burns to the ground. The markings on his back signify the high title he holds in his clan. His eyes focused with rage as the huts collapse around him. He lets out a tremendous roar that can be heard for miles.

CHAPTER 19

INT. LAILOKEN'S CAVE-UNA'S ROOM

The heat from the small fire in the center of the room keeps Una warm as she lies on her grass bed thinking about what her father told Michael. She tries not to cry.

Michael enters the room and lies down behind her. Wrapping his arm around her, he gently pushes his head close to her neck and breathes her scent in deeply.

UNA

Turns to Michael with concern:

"You don't have to fight him. We can leave this place and make a new home somewhere else."

Michael considers her words, but knows the truth of such things. Michael holds Una close to him.

MICHAEL

"I don't want to fight something like that, but I may not

have a choice. We could leave, but this darkness will not. It will follow us to the ends of the world."

UNA

Tears run down her cheeks:

"I don't want to lose you."

They lay completely down in the bed. Michael holds Una as she cries. Michael contemplates the task that has been set before him. His weapons lay in a neat pile across from them. The fires light reflects off the metal of the T.D.B.

EXT. THE FOREST

The morning dew drips from the leaves and shimmers against the dense fog that blankets the forest. The entrance to the cave can barely be seen through the thick brush.

INT. LAILOKEN'S CAVE- THE SPELL ROOM

The work table sits idle. No brewing potions or elixirs this day. No burning torches, just the silence and darkness of the early morning. Lailoken sits in the spell room meditating and building his strength in case he may need it in the battle to come.

The focus expressed through the creases in his brow is fierce as the beads of sweat roll down his body. His eyes flick wide open. He quickly stands up and runs to Una's room to get Michael.

The air is thick with oppression and the stink of hell.

INT. LAILOKEN'S CAVE-UNA'S ROOM

Lailoken rushes into the room to wake Michael. The old man reaches out to shake Michael's arm gently but firmly.

LAILOKEN

"Is é an olc ar gar!"

(The evil one is near!)

The couple immediately sits up. The light sleep was barely able to hold them in its webs. Una turns to face the father of her unborn child with worry in her heart and mind.

MICHAEL

"You must go with your father and get as far away from here as you can."

Michael kisses her deeply and holds his forehead to hers:

"I love you."

Michael helps Una up. She looks at him with tears brimming in her eyes trying not to let the tears fall with little success. The tears roll down her cheek, but Michael catches them and wipes them away.

UNA

"Please come back to me."

Knowing that time is short, Lailoken takes Una and they leave the cave. Michael gets dressed and checks to see if all of his gear still works before he heads outside to wait for the demon.

EXT. OUSIDE LAILOKEN'S CAVE

Just outside the entrance, Michael looks back and above the entrance of the cave. Further up the mountain side he can see Lailoken and Una running into the forest and out of sight.

A violent wind demands the attention of Michael and he looks forward to find a man walking towards him. The features of the man are lost within the mist. A bird caws in the distance.

The branches on the forest ground shatter under his step. The grass and trees wither around him as he makes his way closer to Michael. Only meters away the demon's silhouetted figure gives way to more detail. With every step the man becomes more and more visible.

Michael looks on in disbelief as the man comes out of the dense fog and into focus. He realizes that this is the same man from France and Germany. Michael recognizes the ancient evil man.

MICHAEL

Whispering to himself:

"I don't fucking believe it!"

The shock of the realization that the ancient demon is the same man that has complete control of the world government and is the same man that killed his parents, completely stuns Michael for a moment. The demon draws near closing the distance between them.

Regaining his wits, Michael charges at Belial, punching him in the face with a small amount of enhanced energy in his strike to test the waters. A shock wave erupts from the blow. Michael is shocked when Belial is unfazed by his attack. Michael jumps back and focuses his energy to lift a boulder and smash it over Belial. The dark man is knocked back a few steps, then in a rage he rushes Michael, punching him in the gut full force, stealing the wind out from his lungs and lifting him into the air. Michael feels Belial grab his collar. Michael is pulled into his knee lift. A burst of stabbing pain that causes him to see a blinding white light as he is flung away like a ragdoll into the trunk of a tree.

Belial looks up the mountain in the direction that Lailoken and Una had escaped and proceeds to follow them.

Michael writhes on the ground in pain and after a few moments he staggers to his feet. He notices that Belial is already making his way up the mountain.

CHAPTER 20

EXT. MOUNTAIN WOODS

Una and her father make their way up the steep mountain. Lailoken, looks back to find that, Belial is following them.

LAILOKEN

Pushes Una away:

"Go! Get as far away as you can!"

Lailoken uses his life's energy to coax the trees to create a wall to slow Belial, but they just wither and die when his aura touches them. Lailoken can see Michael running up the mountain fast to catch up to Belial. The old mage spreads his arms and slowly makes a circle before they meet at his chest. He brings them together to strike the ground, causing a pillar of stone to shoot up through the damp earth to collide with Belial's jaw, knocking him up and back. Seeing that his stall tactic worked, Lailoken moves to catch up to Una.

Michael bolts up to the air born demon. He waits until Belial is right above him, then he lifts his arm, uses his energy to blast Belial higher into the air before firing off a few rounds from his gun into the back of the demon.

Belial hits the ground and rolls down the mountain for a couple of meters before hopping up and on to his feet. The gashes from where the metal slugs had exited his body are already closing up leaving only a dark viscous substance that must be the things blood.

BELIAL

"Tá an Bás an t-aon bhealach amach!"

(Death is your only way out!)

Belial charges up the mountain. Michael leaps over the demon, takes hold of his head in mid air and shoots him in the face at point blank range. Michael uses the momentum of his leap to slam the demons head into the ground.

MICHAEL

Screaming:

"Then this is war!"

Michael begins to smash Belial's face in a blind rage. Belial lies there motionless, a bloody mess among the leaves and grass. Michael stands up and manages to wipe some of the dark blood from his face. His breathing is labored as he looks at Belial for a moment and begins to head up the mountain.

As Michael walks up the steep incline to meet up with Una and her father, Belial rises and uses his energy to blast the hell out of Michael, causing him to be thrown up the mountain. Michael slams into five trees before he crashes to the ground.

Belial sprints full speed at Michael and kicks him in the chest with all of his might. The blow sends Michael hurdling up, and out the forest.

EXT. GRASSY MOUNTAIN SUMMIT

Una hears the blast and turns around to see Michael flying out of the forest, tumbling head over heels through the air before crashing violently to the ground.

UNA

Collapses to the ground and screams:

"Michael!"

Lailoken watches as Belial walks out into the clearing. Una watches as Michael gets up and charges at Belial firing shot after shot from his gun.

Belial dodges the projectiles then disappears into thin air causing Michael to pause for a moment in confusion. Then the demon elf re-appears right in front of Michael palming him by the jaw, holding his mouth shut and begins to hammer him in the gut until Michael hangs limp. Belial releases Michael, watching as he falls limply to the ground. A gentle rumble fills the air as tiny droplets of rain fall from the sky. Una watches in painful horror as Michael lies on the damp ground motionless.

UNA

"No!"

Lailoken watches as it seems that there is nothing that can be done to stop Belial. The old mage moves in front of his daughter to protect her.

LAILOKEN

Shaking head:

"It can't be over yet."

Una and her father back away from the ancient demon putting them closer to the edge of the mountain.

With only a meter and half now separating father and daughter from certain death, Belial reaches out for Lailoken with an energy blast primed. Like a black flash, Michael tackles Belial, causing the blast to be shot into the air as they both go over the edge.

CHAPTER 21

EXT. SIDE OF THE MOUNTAIN

As they fall, Michael delivers a series of heavily enhanced punches that rock the head of Belial. Through the strikes Belial can see Lailoken and Una looking over the edge as he and Michael plummet to the rocky shores below.

As the two combatants struggle, Michael can see that they are quickly approaching a narrow cliff face that is jutting out from the cliff side. Michael uses Belial as a shield as they smash into a narrow ledge, shattering it in to thousands of jagged pieces. Michael continues to slam his elbow in the temple and the bridge of the nose of his enemy.

MICHAEL

Screaming:

"I won't let you go on!"

The ground fast approaches filling up the view of Michael's vision. Michael uses an energy push to slam Belial into the ground and at the same time slow his own decent to safe and manageable fall.

EXT. BASE OF THE MOUNTAIN

The ground explodes displacing the earth as Belial smashes into it. While upside down in the air, Michael begins to fire on Belial with his gun, each round penetrates Belial's chest and abdomen, shredding his flesh. Michael lands and continues to shoot Belial.

Frustrated, Belial lets out a primal roar then shoots into the air, further shattering the stones beneath him and deepening the crater he was lying in. He puts some distance between him and Michael. The immortal starts to regenerate. Belial looks at Michael with hateful eyes. After a moment the demon begins to laugh at Michael as his wounds close and the bleeding stops. Michael looks at Belial and swings his head from side to side, cracking his neck in preparation for the next round. The two men charge each other howling fierce battle cries. They both punch each other in the face while Belial's stray energy blast finally falls and explodes behind them. More shock waves erupts from their blows.

Dazed, Michael leans forward with another elbow strike to Belial's face. Belial gives Michael a stiff front kick to the gut then follows it up with a devastating spinning back fist nearly taking off Michaels head.

Before Michael can recover, Belial grabs him by the throat and begins to slowly squeeze. Michael struggles to break free then lifts his gun under the demon's chin and squeezes the trigger rapidly until the bullets break through the demon's skull. Repositioning the Equalizer, Michael begins to shoot Belial in the face.

Belial lets go of Michael and drops back a few steps. Michael pulls his hands back imitating his favorite video game. He charges a massive energy blast.

Belial lunges to counter attack but Michael fires the energy ball at the demon with perfect timing. The dense ball collides with Belial, explodes in a flash of fire and lightning, sending Belial sailing through the air for several meters before he crashes to the ground. The force of the impact is so great that Belial slides on the jagged rocks with such force that his body carves a furrow in the ground for a few meters. The demon rises to his feet.

BELIAL

"Ní féidir leat mé a mharú. Tá mé bás a fháil."

(You can't kill me. I'm immortal.)

Michael laughs, blood coats his teeth then he pulls out is A.X.L. and ignites it. The metal rod slides out in a flash of movement and begins to spin. The lasers whirl around as they heat up and evaporate the rain droplets that comes into contact with it.

MICHAEL

"Bímis féach an féidir leat bheith beo gan do do cheann."

(Let us see if you can live without your head.)

EXT. GRASSY MOUNTAIN-EDGE

Una leans over the mountain and watches as the battle continues on the shore below. She holds her belly. The child in her womb feels like it is fighting alongside its father. Lailoken places his hand on her shoulder and watches with her.

EXT. BASE OF THE MOUNTAIN

Michael charges at Belial and begins to fire a series of shots at the devilish creature. A few shots hit home digging through the center mass of Belial, while the higher shots tear away pieces of his neck. Michael burns a flash of magnesium blinding his opponent then jumps and plants a well aimed flying sidekick to Belial's throat knocking the terrible man off balance.

Michael swings his A.X.L. at Belial aiming for the head, but with his sight returning, Belial catches Michael's hand. Michael lifts his gun and uppercuts Belial. As the blow connects he shoots him in the jaw causing the demon's head to violently rock back. Belial releases Michael as he takes a few steps back to regain his balance and fires an energy ball. Michael flips through the air to dodge it. The energy ball explodes behind Michael.

Michael takes a swing at Belial, but the demon disappears and re-appears behind him then kicks Michael in the back of the head. It was like the sun exploded his mind. Michael is pushed forward from the force of the blinding blow. He rolls out to hop back on his feet and face Belial. Before Michael can recover, Belial grabs him by the lapel of his coat, punching him in the face multiple times before charging an energy ball and letting it rip into Michael's chest, cracking his body armor and sending him flying.

While in mid air, Michael gains some control, flips his body to keep from landing on his head and causing further damage. Once Michael lands, Belial is already on the offensive, charging at him. Michael runs at Belial to meet him head on. Running full speed, Michael leaps forward and uses his head to smash the nose of Belial. Spinning full circle, Michael maneuvers his A.X.L. in a low swing slicing off Belial's leading leg. With nothing to support his weight, Belial drops to the ground. He tries to pick himself up and in an instant, his right arm is hacked off and sent flying in a wave of gore.

Belial looks up at Michael, his eyes wide with actual fear for his life. Michael peers down at the bloody man thing while raising his laser sword above his head.

MICHAEL

Ready to take off Belial's head:

"Now, about that head."

As Michael is about to take off the head of the beaten demon a swirling black ripple appears behind him sucking up the surrounding rocks and other debris. Michael is caught off guard. He has to deactivate his weapon to try and regain his balance. Feeling that he is being sucked backward toward the unknown danger, Michael crouches down to grab for something, anything to keep his feet on the ground. Realizing that he cannot hold his ground any longer, Michael looks up at Una.

EXT. GRASSY MOUNTAIN-EDGE

Una watches Michael as he puts his hand to his heart and raises it up to her before he is violently sucked into the wormhole.

EXT. GRASSY MOUNTAIN-BASE

Belial drops in exhaustion, relieved that the fight is over and he still has his life. He looks up to see Lailoken looking back down at him. The beaten demon closes his eyes and breathes deeply trying to heal his wounds. He takes one more look at Lailoken before he closes his eyes to rest and heal what parts of his body he can. A crow caws into the early morning air.

EXT. GRASSY MOUNTAIN-EDGE

Una looks at her father. The deep pain in her eyes reaches his heart. She drops to the soggy grass weeping for her love.

UNA

Sobbing:

"What did the dark one do to him?"

LAILOKEN

Confused:

"That was not his power."

Lailoken looks down at Una dumbfounded:

"That was my summoning rift."

Una looks at her father, her tears frozen in her eyes. Una looks down at her belly thinking of her their child. Michael may not be around to see its first steps or watch as it grows. She looks back at her father with a pleading expression. He kneels down to her meeting her sorrowful eyes and makes a silent promise.

EXT. WASTELAND

Michael falls out of the hole in space. He looks up to find that the sky is blood red. The vibrant blue lightning crackles as it tears through the crimson clouds. The buildings in the distance are destroyed and crumbling. His eyes try desperately to adjust to his new surroundings. He can see blobs of shadowy figures all around him then a bright flash like a solar flare erupts around him.

BOOK 2

CHAPTER 1
PART 2

INT. HOUSE-LITTLE GIRLS ROOM-DEC. 22, 2113

The room is quiet and peaceful as little Frost colors on a page in one of her father's books. Her doodles are so colorful and vibrant. The yellow-orange light from outside shimmers through the window and dances across the little girls face as she is lost in her own world, unaware that the lives of many people outside are coming to an end.

Her father, Kaiden burst through the door in a panic, pauses for what seems like a lifetime to locate his daughter, then snatches the five year old girl up and heads back out the room.

KAIDEN

Panic and fear stressing his voice:

"Come on honey we have to go."

FROST

"Where are we going daddy?"

INT.INSIDE THE HOUSE-HOUSE

Kaiden cradles Frost like a football as he sprints down the steps. He can see the few bags his wife has packed waiting by the front door, but she is nowhere to be found.

KAIDEN

Running down the steps yelling up at his wife:

"Honey, forget the other bags! We have to go now!"

INT. MASTER BEDROOM-HOUSE

Upstairs, the master bedroom lay in shambles as Fionala rushes to gather their things. She pauses and looks at the holo screen in disbelief. The chaos unfolding outside seems like it leaped right out of a crazy man's wild nightmare. She can see the carnage while it is being described by the bloody news man.

NEWS MAN

Hiding behind the news van while the military battle the horrific horde behind him:

"I have just been informed that anyone still in the city should evacuate immediately! I repeat; if you are still in the city evacuate immediately! The creatures emerging from the gate are extremely dangerous!"

A tank can be seen hurdling toward the frantic newscaster as he is unaware of his own death approaching.

Fionala gasps as the tank smashes the news van and the man hiding behind it. The holo camera drops to the ground with a thud, cracking the lens, but showing a perfect view of the hordes marching forward and through the clouds of dust and debris.

Fionala brushes her long dark hair back behind her mildly pointed ears and stares at the display of her cell phone worried. She yells back at her husband.

FIONALA

"I can't get a hold of my nephew!"

INT. FRONT DOOR-HOUSE

Standing at the doorway pulling the straps of the bags over his shoulder Kaiden yells up the stairway at his wife. The screams emanating from beyond the front door are getting more frantic, more desperate as the chaos spreads through the city blocks like a plague.

KAIDEN

"I'm sure Michael has already left the city! C'mon we have to get out of here now!"

Fionala comes running down the steps. Her tears have ruined the make up around her eyes forming black streaks that run down her face.

Looking up at her father worried:

"Daddy what's going on?!"

Kaiden swings the door open and dashes outside carrying the small girl in his arms. An explosion rocks a sky scrapper in the heart of the city, causing its top half to come crashing down. The destroyed building smashes into office buildings before it finally crumbles to the ground smashing everything and everyone below it. Kaiden hears a loud floosh from above and spots two dozen ISOS Jets speeding through the sky firing Sparrow missiles. He follows the screeching ballistics across the sky and freezes in bone chilling terror at the sight of the Leviathans that fill the upper atmosphere like a swarm of locust. The missiles explode on impact in a spectacular white hot flash of fire, but the giant creatures seem to only be inconvenienced by the highly explosive rockets.

Frost shrieks in terror at the horrors before her eyes. Her world had always been so fluffy and full of hope until this very moment when it all burns down around her.

EXT. CITY STREET

The armored dragons swirl through the sky, like ribbons dancing in the wind. The fighter jets move in to engage them. The jets to the rear of the formation break away to move into flanking positions while the fighters at the head fire their mounted automatic pulse guns into the floating slithering mass of creatures. The creatures roar with every shot that pelts their tuff hides. The monsters riding the giant beasts steer the dragons into a defensive formation and begin their counter attack against the fighter jets.

The city is completely decimated as the torrent of monsters rampage through the streets murdering anyone they come across. Smoke fills the air for miles and blocks out the light from the sinking sun, leaving the world below in a grey fog. Kaiden opens the door to the sky car and throws Frost inside not worrying about buckling her in then he makes his way to the driver seat.

INT. SKY CAR-CITY STREET

A jet crashes to the ground a few yards away from the house throwing pavement and metal in every direction. Shrapnel from the downed plane smashes through the rear window in a loud crash. Frost screams in terror as beads of glass rain down around her. The blackened pieces of metal smacks into the side of Kaiden's face burning it instantly, blistering and melting his skin. He grabs his face in pain careful not to touch his skin fearing that he would do more damage to the side of his face. He looks in to the rearview mirror to inspect the damage of his bloody and blistered face, but movement from the dust cloud yanks at his attention.

KAIDEN

"Jesus!"

Kaiden turns and looks through the busted rear window, where he can see a mob of creatures marching down the street. There must be hundreds of them, but he can't tell through the twisted burning wreck of a plane.

KAIDEN

"What the fuck is that?"

He turns and looks back at the house to try and hurry his wife along but his heart stops when he finds Fionala partially sprawled on the ground and on the front step motionless. Dark crimson Blood dribbles from her head to the concrete step.

KAIDEN

"Fionala! Fionala get up!"

FROST

Crying:

"Daddy I'm scared!"

Thinking his wife dead, Kaiden closes the doors, lowers the wings to the car and initiates the vertical takeoff. The engines heat up with a low whine that grows with speed. Frost presses herself against the window to see her mother shakily climbing to her feet.

EXT. CITY STREET-FRONT OF HOUSE

Fionala stumbles to her feet dazed and confused. She looks for her husband and daughter then panics when she finds neither where she had last seen them. The smoke from the burning jet fuel feels like acid in her lungs and she coughs trying to catch her breath. She knew the car was there before the jet crashed. Frantically, she searches then she looks up and her heart breaks to see her daughter beating on the window crying while looking down at her, as the car rises into the air.

FIONALA

Crying:

"I love you baby girl! Mommy will always love you!"

INT. SKY CAR

The tears burn and skew the view of her mother. It only causes Frost to cry harder. A few short moments later the mass of monsters reach her mother and she is swallowed up by the pack of beasts. With tears frozen by terror, Frost screams in fear for her mother. Turning to her father while glaring out the window she beats on him so hard that he jerks the yoke to the side and narrowly misses a row of homes.

FROST

"Go back! Help mommy! What are you doing? Help mommy!"

A monstrous sky dragon swoops toward the car, mouth a gape and ready to devour the car and its occupants. A missile explodes in the dragon's face creating a crater of flesh on the side of its head causing it to veer hard to the side and crash through the homes on the other side of the street. Seeing his opening Kaiden takes off at full speed leaving Frost's entire world behind.

CHAPTER 2

INT. SUBTERRANEAN CAVE-NINETEEN YEARS LATER

A much older Frost wakes up in a cold sweat. Her black tattered jump suit is drenched and clings to her body. She unzips the top half and peels her shoulders out of the sleeveless top, folds it down around her waist and uses a belt to secure it in place. She grabs an old undershirt and pulls it over her head then tucks it into the belt. Her short dark hair hangs down around her violet eyes. The strands cling to one another in little hanging spikes. The cavity she calls her room is damp. The torches mounted to the walls burn bright casting an orange glow on the dark limestone rocks. The voices emanating from beyond her room are low, but it is obvious they are all in distress. Nothing new. The people of her clan argue all the time, but the hint of true panic is what catches her ear.

INT. SUBTERRANEAN CAVE-MEETING CHAMBER

The torches mounted on the pillars fight off the darkness that threatens to overtake the circular meeting room. The elders of the clan stand huddled together and argue among themselves.

KYLE

Shouting over the masses:

"When have our scouts ever let us down? The death squads are two days away and we are sitting here fighting with each other when we should be united. We are doing their job for them."

Frost stands in an archway listening to the others. She can't help but notice that some are in full body armor, while others are just wearing the old grey and black military uniforms they scavenged from old strongholds.

Kaiden sits in his chair listening with a false calm masking his face. His bald head gleams with beads of sweat in the fire light. His graying beard is long and unkempt with the exception of where he no longer grows hair on his face.

KAIDEN

"I have already sent out scouts to relay the message to the tribe leaders. They should be here by the end of the day with their answer. Until then we should leave this place and find another clan to fortify ourselves."

FROST

Defiant in her tone:

"So, you are suggesting that we run from this threat and abandon all that we have worked for all these years?"

KAIDEN

"Yes. That is exactly what I'm saying we do."

Frost steps through the crowd of people so that she can look her father in the eye. The wound left by the loss of her mother only grew and festered through the years fueling her resentment toward her father.

FROST

"Run away? I shouldn't expect much more from a man who left his wife to die while he saved his own ass."

The people stop shouting and stand idle and in shock while Frost belittles her father. Many of the people that were watching the debate grab their children and head to their dwellings to pack their belongings.

KAIDEN

A tired anger lines his voice:

"I had to do what was necessary to save you, and I will continue to do what is necessary to save others."

Frost can tell that her father is furious, but desperately trying to keep a level head to save face with his fellow elders. He knows that she has had the dream again. Most days she's content to ignore him, but she only bites his head off when she has had the nightmare.

FROST

"You had more than enough time to get her! You chose to be a coward!"

Red faced, Kaiden slams his fist on the arm of his chair cracking it. The vein in his forehead nearly burst out of his skin. Spittle flies from his mouth as he speaks.

KAIDEN

"I have to live with my decisions every goddamn day!"

FROST

Calmly walking away:

"As do I."

CHAPTER 3

EXT. WASTELAND

The darkness of the night encloses the city in shadow. The red sky crackles with lightning, briefly illuminating the devastated landscape. The glow from the full moon casts a gray purple hue through the clouds that hang low and mesh together, building in mass over the landscape. The dark city swallows up any residual light shared by the bright sphere above. Lightning strikes a tall sky scraper in the distance igniting the trash that litters its upper floors. The faint glow can be seen for miles. The wind howls like a banshee through shattered windows and hollow buildings. The sound is almost like the lost souls that once lived in its buildings and walked its streets are crying from whatever hell they dwell in now.

Two lone scouts run for their lives over the rooftops. After witnessing their unit of six men and women get annihilated by a pack of other worldly monsters, they know that they carry the last hope for their clan. The mission must be completed. They stop and take cover behind an old air ventilation unit to figure out some kind of game plan. Shay readjusts her light armor breast plate and elbow pads over her dark blue jumpsuit. Her bright red hair spills over her goggles frustrating her. Shay repositions the goggles so that they hold the strands of hair in place rather than having them whipped around by the wind. The thunderous lightning strikes again, and for a moment it seems as if the sun has made a brief appearance on this night. The glow of the Lightning illuminates the former metropolis that rests like a scar on the surface of the earth like so many others around the world.

EXT. ROOFTOP-WASTELAND

Brushing her red hair away from her face and back under her goggles, Shay catches her breath to speak. The lack of breath makes her Irish brogue that much harder to understand

SHAY

"What the fuck was that thing?"

William lifts his head to peer over the old rusted air unit to make sure they haven't been followed. His face is flush from running nonstop. He runs his hand over his hair in an attempt to keep the sweat from dripping into his eyes. The stubble of his blonde beard glistens with beads of sweat.

WILLIAM

"I have no clue. I've never seen one that big."

William's eyes dart back and forth, getting his bearings and marking their position on his mental map. He pulls the sleek sack on his back around to his waist for easy access.

WILLIAM CONT'D

"We are four hours away from H.Q. take the instructions and go on ahead."

He pushes the capsule containing the coordinates to the rendezvous in Shay's palm. The few remaining pockets of human resistances have slowly been disappearing all around the world. The handful of military instillations knew it would only be a matter of time before every man, woman and child would be exterminated, so they sent out a call to arms. The powers that be felt it would be better to die on their feet. Resistances all around the world heard the same call and all would meet at their respective military strongholds for their last stand.

SHAY

"What the hell are you doing? You can't be thinking about going up against that thing!"

WILLIAM

"If I don't do something to stall that beast, it will just follow us all the way back. We have no choice."

WILLIAM CONT'D

Looking over the air unit:

"Once you hit the ground don't stop."

Shay lays a gentle hand on William's shoulder, silencing him. He looks at her. His blue eyes are so bright and it's like she is seeing him for the time ever. Moisture blurs her vision of him and she quickly blinks it away. She doesn't want to forget his face. Pulling William to her lips she kisses him deeply. She rests her head on his as a single tear rolls down her cheek and without further pause she begins inching toward the edge of the building. She looks down and then back at her lover.

SHAY

"Be careful. I'll see you at home."

A loud screeching roar echoes through the empty buildings assaulting Shays ears from all sides. The wretched relentless thing draws closer.

They both know that he will not survive the encounter and so, they share one final glance. Shay can hear the thing scaling the tall building. Its bone talons scrape against the concrete façade as the decaying monster scrambles for purchase.

WILLIAM

"Yeah. Now Go!"

Lightning branches out across the sky as Shay leaps off of the building, through the shattered wall of the adjacent high rise, rolls once as she hits the floor and bolts toward the nearest exit.

WILLIAM

"I really didn't feel like dying today."

William stands up and turns in the general direction of the creature. He waits. The charged air around him smells of ozone as he gathers his focus. The creature screams again and he knows it's getting close. He can hear the scuttling of the deformed creatures five legs as it makes its way up to the roof.

WILLIAM CONT'D

"If I can keep that thing from getting to her then it's all good. I love you baby. I hope you know that."

The creature's piercing screams echo through the restless air as it climbs onto the roof like a monster out of a terrible dream.

The almost human figure spider walks its way toward William. The lightning flashes and William can see that its contorted body looks like it's been almost ripped in half. One of its heads dangles in between two of its arms, while the other is buried somewhere in its body. Its barbed tail whips around through a giant gash in its stomach. It's as if someone took a man, broke his back and the man had no choice but to walk upside down on his hands and feet.

William can tell that this manticore has been around for a long time. Most of its flesh had rotted away and the parasite's thin sinew-like tentacles, can be seen whirling about wildly through the holes in the flesh.

WILLIAM

Bracing for the battle:

"Come on you ugly fuck!"

A bolt of lightning streaks down from the sky and in to William's raised hand fueling him. The massive jolt of energy rips through his body with such force that the concussive shockwave vaporizes the old A/C unit. The Manticore digs its boney forelimbs into the stone of the roof to keep from being blown off by the force of the explosion. William leaps forward to engage the deadly beast.

EXT. RUNDOWN BUILDING/WASTELAND

Shay runs like the wind through the buildings corroded interior. She jumps through a broken window and onto a half burnt street lamp that crumbles under her small frame. Shay jumps off the rotted pole just before it smashes to pieces on the hard pavement.

Behind her, in the distance, a massive electrical explosion rocks the building where she had last seen William. She doesn't look back. The rumbling of the tall apartment building is enough to tell her that all she will see is the building disappearing in a cloud of debris. With hot tears in her eyes, Shay bolts into the darkness.

INT. SUBTERRANEAN CAVE-FROST'S ROOM

Frost sits on the stone and grass bed near the far wall of her chamber, running a wet stone along the blade of her sword. She is dressed in her full light armor. Her battered shoulder and elbow pads sport dents and deep scratches from years of hard use. The fires light reflects off of the blade and dances around the room with each practiced stroke.

Kaiden enters the room fired up from their exchange in the main the meeting room. His face is a mask of anger hiding the deep sorrow that eats away at his heart.

KAIDEN

"What the hell is your problem?"

Frost lifts only her eyes to look at him and continues to sharpen her sword, but now there is extra attitude with every stroke. Her disgust from earlier has turned in to a cold anger and some regret. She knows her father meant well, but she can't forgive the fact that he focused on saving his own ass instead of the life of her mother.

KAIDEN CONT'D

"If you feel that you have all the answers, let's hear it!"

Frost says nothing as she continues to sharpen her blade. She looks down to monitor her progress and test the edge of the sword. Ever since she joined the core when she was fifteen years old, a full year before the required age, she had spent many days dreaming of leaving with or finding another clan of like-minded people to take the fight to the human like monsters that hunt them down like dogs.

KAIDEN CONT'D

"If you want to fight and die needlessly then go ahead. I'm tired of being the focus of your anger. You know what? Go on! Get the fuck out of here tough guy!"

Frost shoots up from her seated position so fast that

Kaiden barely had enough time to flinch. As angry as she is at the moment she could take the fight to her father. Her left hand glows with blue mist like energy. She releases her talent, feeling almost ashamed. Kaiden looks her in her eyes, like he is searching her soul for the love she had for him as a child, before the world ended. Not finding what he was looking for he shakes his head in disappointment.

Frost takes her father's gesture as complete rejection, though she had been the one rejecting him throughout the years. Feeling her anger cresting again, she marches out the room before she loses control. Kaiden stands in the small dimly lit room silent as his daughter walks out. He feels he should say something to fix the situation, but he knows it wouldn't make a difference. All he wanted to do was apologize and hug his last surviving family member; his only daughter. He can feel what's left of his heart break away.

INT. EXIT HALL- SUB-CAVE

Frost looks out into the blood red sky. The Massive clouds that clump together in the distance look ominous. She can't help but think that the state of the world is a direct reflection of the emptiness she feels. She loves her father, but that love had been muted that day she watched her mother die from the window of their car. The passing years didn't heal her pain; it made her indifferent towards her father. Not being able to stand the cramped living conditions of the cave for another minute she decides to leave for a few days. She takes three steps then stops when she spots Shay emerging from the darkness.

Shay slows to a jog as she approaches the mouth of the subterranean cave. She's drenched in so much sweat that her navy blue suit drips with every step. Her hair hangs in saturated strands around her face and neck. Her haunted eyes lock on to Frost. She takes a moment to catch her breath. Frost realizes that the rest of squad isn't with her. Good. Now she has an excuse to disappear for a couple of days.

SHAY

"Where's your father?"

FROST

"Inside. Probably still being a giant ass."

Shay rolls her eyes. She can't believe that they are at it again at a time when it's make it or break it. She smiles as not to upset her best friend then she jogs down the entrance of the cave and fades into the darkness of its halls. Her boiled rubber sole shoes make only the slightest of sounds.

FROST CONT'D

"… And a Coward."

Frost heads into the wasteland heedless of the coming storm.

INT. SUB-CAVE-KAIDEN'S CHAMBERS

The dark room is barely illuminated by the torches in the hall. The muffled sounds of the night crew patrolling the halls, playing cards or doing anything to keep their minds off of what the latest reports will bring sounds harsh to the old man's ears. Kaiden sits in the dark brooding over what has just transpired between himself and his daughter. On one hand he feels that she is a spoiled sanctimonious brat whose ass is in need of a good kicking and on the other, he wants nothing more than to hold his baby girl in his arms. He would love to just take her in his arms and let her know how much the choices he had to make kills him every minute of every day, but she would never let him that close. Tired from thinking too much, he closes his eyes. He feels something warm trickle down his cheeks and roll over his upper lip. The salt from his tears catches him by surprise and then the flood gates open and he weeps.

INT. SUB. CAVE

Shay runs through the halls peering in to every important room looking for Kaiden. She's shouting for him. The noise stirs the sleeping families and off duty soldiers. The urgent inflection of her voice causes those listening to perk up and leave the webs of slumber behind.

Kaiden wipes the tears from his face and takes deep breaths to steady his nerves. No one needs to see him this way. She pokes her head in to his room to see if he is there but can see nothing. She keeps moving.

SHAY

"Kaiden where are you?"

KAIDEN

"I'm in here."

Shay whips around and heads back to the elder's room. She moves so fast to turn in to the archway that she is caught off guard when she almost collides with the man making his way out of the room. She steps back and is surprised that he didn't even try to get out of the way. It was like he didn't notice. She recovers quickly then salutes the tired looking man.

SHAY

"Sir, we have less time than we originally thought."

A look of pained grief creeps its way on to Kaiden's dejected expression. For a moment she wonders what had happened, but those thoughts can wait.

SHAY CONT'D

"Some of the other tribes have already been wiped out or have left to the rendezvous. We're practically alone out here."

The aged man pinches the bridge of his nose with his thumb and index finger.

KAIDEN

"What's the situation?"

SHAY

"From the twenty tribes in this area there are only eight

left. Their leaders have agreed to the meeting area and some are already en route. Most are already there."

KAIDEN

"Where are the other scouts?"

The question slaps Shay in the face. She almost loses her professional calm to grief about what had happened to her team and to William. Kaiden notices the almost imperceptible shift and the pains of his personal battles are replace with dread for the families he looks after.

SHAY

"I'm the only one left, Sir."

Kaiden exits the tiny door way in haste and heads toward the main hall with Shay in tow. A soldier stands at a junction with a look of barely controlled anger mingled with terror. As Kaiden approaches him he points to the man.

KAIDEN

"We must get everyone out of here now."

Shay leans forward as she tries to keep pace with the Commanding elder.

SHAY

"Where was Frost headed?"

The old man's head perks up and he nearly breaks his stride for just a moment but he continues walking with purpose.

KAIDEN

Sighs heavily:

> "I told her to leave."

SHAY

Outraged:

> "You sent her out there on her own? She's our best
> soldier! Not to mention your only child!"

*They enter the main bunker full of support and guard staff. The
men and women rise to attention. Some were already getting
suited up and ready to get the families on the move. The
soldiers salute.*

KAIDEN

> "We must get everyone to safety."

INT. SUB. CAVE

*The cave and all of its chambers are alive with activity.
The people scramble franticly to collect their things and gather
their children. They only pack what is essential for survival
and nothing more. In the chaos Shay, with a small backpack
filled with supplies approaches Kaiden.*

SHAY

> "Sir, we have to get Frost."

KAIDEN

"If you wish to go and find her, knock yourself out."

Shay stuffs an extra canteen of water and a hand full of energy bars in her bag and begins to walk down the steps and in to the main hall. As she pushes her way through the crowd of people she is completely shocked that they have both taken things this far. She was never one to pick a side in Frost's and Kaiden's arguments, but this time she must admit that the man who took her in as his own is being completely stubborn.

SHAY

"Unbelievable!"

Shay picks up a crying child and hands him off to his mother who is so frazzled she sets the young toddler back down to gather more of her belongings. Shay walks to the hall that leads outside the cave. Before she leaves, she takes one last look at the people running around like headless chickens feeling sick to her stomach. The adults here are all traumatized. Their lives had come to a shattering halt when the world ended and their children don't know a life outside of a cave or a bunker. They all will grow up knowing only death. That is of course if they get the chance to grow up. She notices Kaiden walking back to the living chambers. His head hung low and shoulders slumped. Shaking her head in disappointment, Shay turns around and exits the cave.

CHAPTER 4

EXT. WASTELAND

Frost sneaks through the forgotten city, being careful to keep to the shadows of the broken buildings. A noise in the distance stops her dead in her tracks. She evaluates her surroundings before moving forward. She hears the noise again only louder this time. She must be getting close. Again, the noise and she realizes that she's hearing a human groan. She knows that she must use caution no matter how safe the environment around her may seem. As she silently moves closer to the pained sounds, she silently draws her sword from its sheath. A shuffling noise can be heard around the next turn. She presses herself against the wall and peeks around the corner. She can see nothing. The noises are coming from what used to be a floral shop, but now stands as a ghostly shell. Frost turns the corner and slowly makes her way inside the small building, ready to kill whatever she may find.

Once inside she surveys the small shop. Everything is dark, but she can see a pair of boots behind a rusted display case. The person they belong to is writhing in pain. Silently she creeps closer. Poised and ready to kill at the slightest hint of a threat. She is caught completely off guard to find, William propped against a wall and who is obviously mortally wounded.

Frost runs to him. On closer inspection she can see that there is a growing pool of dark sticky liquid surrounding him. He looks up. The expression on his face was deep fear mingled with anger. His face softens once he realizes it is his friend, Frost.

FROST

"Will, what happened?"

WILLIAM

"These creatures attacked us. There were so many of them."

William tries to sit up but falls back down in pain. Frost looks at his wounds and notices that there is a wide hole straight through his abdomen and he's not just holding the wound to stop the bleeding, he's holding in his guts. Frost notices some small movements near the hole. The squirming worm creatures in the drying blood is a familiar sight and she begins to inch away from the injured man.

WILLIAM CONT'D

"I managed to stop the one that was following, Shay and I. There isn't much time. These…"

William begins to spasm and then falls to the floor. His back begins to arch so far back it brakes with an audible wet crunch. William begins to scream as his body mangles itself. It pains

Frost to realize what's happening to her friend, but she knows there is nothing she can do for the poor man. The manticor parasite has penetrated his spinal cord and is making connections to his brain. Soon he will just be another monster.

Frost steps back not taking her eyes off of William. His body rips itself apart, exposing the creature that is tearing its way out of his flesh. Frost draws her sword and chops off Williams head. It's too late. The creature continues to use his body. Frost backs away, keeping her eyes locked on the monster as it thrashes violently to its feet. The monster wears William like a torn fleshy suit. Bones puncture the skin and the mangled flesh becomes one with the monster. The creature howls and begins to shuffle toward Frost.

Frost charges her sword with electrical energy and slashes at the beast sending high voltage currents through the nervous system that the abomination has adopted as its own.

EXT. WASTELAND

Frost breathes heavily as she stares at the mangled remains of what used to be William. Frost fights back the tears. This isn't the first time she had witnessed a close friend being taken over by one of those hellish parasites and had to finish them off. She stands in the dark shadow of the building offering a moment of silence for her friend before moving on to find a safe place to stay for the night.

INT. SUB.CAVE- KAIDEN'S CHAMBERS

Kaiden gathers his things in the poorly lit room. He can hear scratching in a dark corner. He pauses to inspect the odd sound.

KAIDEN

"Who's there?"

Kaiden walks over to the dark corner of the room expecting to find some small rodent or some other animal. What he finds steals the air from his lungs.

Fionala looking just as she did nineteen years ago walks out from the darkness. She is dressed in black leather with blood red armor across her chest and shoulders. She slowly walks over to the stunned old man. The aging man reaches out for her. His eyes screams of regret and longing for his former wife.

KAIDEN CONT'D

"Is that really you?"

She nods her head in response and leans in to kiss him. Her soft moist lips gently touch his dry and cracked mouth.

SENGI (FIONALA)

"My darling, you're trembling."

Tears stream down the old man's face as he looks into the dark eyes of the woman who cannot be. He moves in and almost crumbles to his knees as he embraces her.

"I've missed you so much. I'm so sorry. I..."

She places her half gloved finger on his lips silencing him. The smile that creases her face sends him aback. He can't help but think that it seems predatory.

SENGI (FIONALA)

"Shhh. It will all be over soon my love."

Screams fill the caverns as the slaughter begins. Kaiden turns his head in surprise and Sengi (Fionala) lets her finger trail its way down Kaiden's chin, past his throat and then traces tiny swirls over his chest. Her eyes begin to water as his gaze meets hers. She drives her fist through his breast plate shattering bone to grab at his heart and then she rips it out. She can't help but cry as she laughs. Kaiden stares at his former wife in shock and horror as she holds the blood pump that was once in his chest. He stumbles then collapses to the cold stone. The thin sheen of moisture that covers his eyes drip out. The tear rolls across the bridge of his nose and then drops to the ground to mingle with his blood.

INT. SUB. CAVE- MAIN HALL

The human inhabitants scream as the demons fill the cave killing all that they pass. They seem to target the children first. They don't kill the young ones. They rip them away from their parents and hand them off into the lamprey mouth of the scaled worm like creatures that follow like loyal dogs behind the larger demons. Sengi looks on in sad sadistic pleasure.

CHAPTER 5

EXT. WASTELAND-HALF BURNED HOUSE

The old run down house sits like a squat troll in the middle of the tall buildings that have long since fallen in on themselves. The windows are shattered and the front door hangs off its hinges. The cursed earth claimed this place long ago. Vegetation grows along the walls inside the house, clinging to the rotting structure like thick spiders webs. Frost wonders if the snaking vines are all that's holding the crumbling place up.

She sits in the darkest corner of the rundown home trying to sleep. She knows the dream will come. The same dream that she has dreamed since the world ended has haunted her for years, but she doesn't fight it this time. She allows herself to drift away.

A soft crunching sound can be heard just outside the house. The light footsteps stirs Frost from her slumber. She crouches on the balls of her feet fully aware and ready to fight. She silently creeps toward the fire blackened glass of a broken window, then peeks out a small crack and sees that there is nothing out of the ordinary. Did she imagine it? The storm has past and the landscape is still dead. What's left of the charred skyscrapers and the once gleaming glass structures stand as the tombstones of a civilization long lost.

The front door falls off of its frame startling Frost. Just as she starts to relax she can see what looks like the rotted head of a horse with fangs poke through the doorway, look around and silently walk into the house. The creature is slight and it seems that the head is just a little too large for its slender frame. The odd intruder is lightly armored with what seems to be bare bones rigged to be shoulder, chest and thigh guards resting over a tattered old world military uniform.

Frost slowly draws her sword and sits in the shadows waiting for the right moment to strike. The thing turns so that its back is now facing Frost as it surveys the room. Frost jumps out of the darkness and swings her sword only to have it deflected by a blur of metal. The thing had turned around to parry Frost's attack. Then it removes the dead demon head to reveal an older lady wearing the demon's hide over an old flight suit. Under the dirt and grime from long exposure to the elements, Frost can see that the woman is very attractive. Her soft features look out of place with the hard reality of the world.

RAYNE

"Whoa! You could have killed me! Who just attacks another person like that? What's wrong with you child?"

Frost steps back in alarm and confusion. She looks the woman over, wondering just where the hell this person had come from.

FROST

"Who the hell walks around with a demon skull on their head? How was I supposed to know you were human?"

Rayne sits on the burnt steps that lead to the upstairs of the rickety old house. She sets the worn skull next to her on the weed covered floor. She looks up at the young woman and smiles.

RAYNE

"Well, shit you're right. Better safe than sorry. The name's Rayne."

Relieved that the lady hasn't tried to eat her yet and letting her guard down, but only a little, Frost nods.

FROST

"I'm Frost."

Rayne holds her hand out. She can see that her smile had barely disarmed the girl, but that was to be expected. Feral humans have been known to attack other humans, but those stories have died down over the years.

RAYNE

"Well nice to meet you Frosty."

FROST

"Don't call me that."

Rayne shrugs as Frost leans over to look out the window checking for less friendly beings that may have seen the odd woman enter the building. Seeing no immediate threats, Frost turns to the older woman.

FROST CONT'D

"Were you following me?"

Rayne stands to stretch her legs and back while running her fingers through her dark dirt clumped hair.

RAYNE

"No. Not really. I saw you come in here some time ago and I thought that maybe you didn't want to be out here all by your lonesome."

FROST

"You look like you've been out here for a while. Where did you come from?"

Rayne lightly walks over to Frost. Her smile widens as she contemplates the question and reflects on the past. She nods as if recalling some memory that related to the situation. She peers out in to the wasteland from the door way, and then points up the stairs to indicate that they should find a better place to relax for the night. The two ladies creep silently up the old rotting steps.

RAYNE

"Well it's kind of a shitty story, but since you asked. I

came from an old military base in what used to be Kentucky. It seemed like a good place to hide out at the time and it was. Fortified and well-armed too. My people were so hell bent on waging a war I knew they couldn't win."

FROST

"You refused to fight?"

Rayne shakes her head disagreeing with the young lady's assessment of her heavily modified tale.

RAYNE

"No. Not at all. I just didn't feel the need to fight recklessly. The commanding officer and I got into it and even though I won, I was thrown into the Brigg."

FROST

"That's bullshit."

Rayne laughs as she recalls the memory of sitting in a dark cell.

RAYNE

"That's what I said, but it is what it is. I've been out here for six winters."

FROST

"Six years? How did you not starve to death?"

RAYNE

"Well when you've been out here as long as I have you learn to like the taste of certain things, monster meat being among them."

Frost shutters at the thought of being forced to eat the disgusting creatures that roam the wastelands.

RAYNE CONT'D

"It tastes like deer. It's very good actually. You'll learn to like it once you stop thinking about it. I call it M & Ms as a joke. Get it? Monster Meat. M & Ms."

The strange woman smiles knowingly at Frost as she takes a bite of some "monster meat". Frost pulls out a canteen and drinks. She offers some water to Rayne as she chuckles.

CHAPTER 6

EXT. DARK FORTRESS

The castle sits like a giant obsidian fortress of alien design over a steep hillside, overlooking another lost human city. The turrets stretch high into the sky with bridges connecting them to one another. The portcullis looks as if it was fashioned from the monstrous skull of a terrifying nephilim with the mouth serving as an entry point.

INT. DARK FORTRESS-THRONE ROOM

Inside the throne room, the black flags hang from the vaulted ceilings. The yellow sigils crisscross on the black material in an ornate pattern signifying the ruling house.

Belial sits on his bone and fire glass throne dressed in fine silks while his generals sit around a large table located near the center of the room. Some dine on the flesh of the braised humans and animals they keep as cattle in the lower levels of the fortress. The dark room is illuminated with a blue tint from the ethereal fire that dances in the large hearth on the far wall. A handsome yet, older looking elf sits at the table. His white robes draped over one shoulder leaving the other bare showing off his tattoos. The fine leather strap holding his sword in place rests firmly wrapped around his torso. Brushing his fine dark hair away from his eyes he speaks.

IZETA

"The humans are planning a unified strike against us my Lord. We have intercepted scouts from several different human tribes that corroborate our claims."

BELIAL

"Let those pathetic animals try."

Isis pulls off her black and red leather gloves and sets them on the table. Her skimpy armored outfit serves as more of a distraction rather than actual protection.

ISIS

"The Manticore hunters have located more human hives just outside the city and infected scores while tearing through others. I would have never thought to use vermin as weapon but, the parasite has proved to be useful after all. Wouldn't you agree Izeta?"

Annoyed that the conversation isn't yielding any actual good information Belial interrupts the siblings before they can enter into one of their frequent verbal battles.

BELIAL

"What of the offspring of Michael? Have they all been

located and destroyed?"

The fine featured demon smiles, but the gesture doesn't reach his eyes.

IZETA

"Sengi performs her task well, my Lord. She has tracked down the last of her kin and is purging them as we speak. We won't have to worry about them anymore."

The huge ornate doors of the room swing open. The others look back to see the half breed Prince Solomn entering the room, clad in his boiled leather armor, dragging a battered human scout behind him. The man's clothes hang from his body in strips. The low moans of the beaten man echo and bounce of the walls of the large circular room. Solomn whips the man toward the front and places him on his knees. The Prince has the man by the back of his neck in an iron grip and props him up to face his father Belial. The Prince salutes his father, then he turns to Izeta and nods in acknowledgment of his former tutor. Izeta nods back with a slight smile in his eyes.

SOLOMN

"Father, forgive my interruption but, this human has information and I think it's something you should hear."

When the man doesn't speak, Solomn clinches his neck causing him to grunt in pain. The man cowers in fear of the monsters glaring at him from their seats. To be so close to the leaders of his enemies fills him with both fear and a sense of utter uselessness.

PAN

"We've been keeping a weapon in our strongholds, capable of mass destruction. My elders plan on using this weapon against you and your kind. They are on their way now to activate it."

The King looks at the small man with annoyed amusement. Growing very tired of his son's interruption and the story from the sad sack of wasted space called a human; Belial thinks of ways to slowly kill the man.

BELIAL

"What weapon could your kind possibly have that we haven't wiped out over the nineteen years this one sided war has been waged?"

The beaten man holds his tongue in defiance of the foul creatures before him. He tries to hold out, but Solomn squeezes his neck using his sharpened claws to puncture and break the skin. Pan Screams in pain and tries to compose himself as bolts of pain rip through his body. Blood trickles down his neck.

PAN

"We have been storing Black Matter warheads that we will use against you."

Isis walks over to the injured man and nods at her nephew. The predatory smile that parts her almost angelic features only serves to unnerve the broken man. Solomn releases his hold. She leans over, exposing her cleavage, and strokes the man's

---

unkempt hair.

ISIS

"Such a good boy you are. Too bad I already have enough pets."

Looking at the big breasted demon with distain in his eyes, Pan spits in her face.

PAN

"I may not get to see the end of this war, but I know that my people will have you all begging for mercy."

Isis stands up straight and wipes the spittle from her eye. She turns toward Belial and raises one eyebrow in a silent question.

BELIAL

"I find it absolutely hilarious that you humans will destroy everything when you cannot overcome a greater force. You cling to hope like maggots cling to a corpse and when that hope is gone you say fuck it all. I love your fighting spirit. You see, it doesn't matter what your kind has hidden or plan to use, because it will all be over very, very soon. Kill him."

The prince freezes and takes hold of the man before him. Solomn had no intention of killing the prisoner. He looked to his old master for support but found only a defeated expression.

SOLOMN

"My Lord, I have already told this man that he may keep his life if he confessed."

Truly disheartened, Izeta looks at his former pupil with pleading eyes. He couldn't bare the sight of watching a child he practically raised be punished for having a heart.

IZETA

"Sorry young one, you can't save them all. They can't even save themselves. Besides, if you tried to save them it would only be a foolish crusade seeing how they can't help but kill each other. If they weren't fighting us, they'd still be fighting each other. In fact, they did much of the work for us in the beginning."

Solomn turns and exits the room. Angered he slams the door shut leaving the man to his fate. Isis turns back to face Pan, smiling and begins to walk around toward the back of the man, making her way full circle around to his front. Taking in his measure of resolve in cold calculation, the She Devil leans in close so that her lips are pressed close to his right ear and whispers softly.

ISIS

"Very rarely does a nearly extinct creature make a comeback. You are a dying breed."

Isis leans back a bit to look Pan in his frightened eyes, peering into his soul. The She Witch kisses Pan while she clinches his throat and crushes his wind pipe. Isis slides her hands up around the suffocating man's head and pushes her thumbs up to the knuckle into his eyes. Pan tries to scream but his throat is smashed shut. The man slumps to the floor. The Hell Hounds that were sitting patiently by the table creep up and proceed to devour the dying man as he fights to breathe.

CHAPTER 7

EXT. WASTELAND

The morning sun begins to rise, illuminating the buildings that clutter the horizon. The scorched towers shade most of the land with their long stretching shadows.

Shay comes to an old broken down home, walks through the door and finds what appears to be an empty house. Confused, she investigates further. All the signs are there, though they've done a fairly good job at concealing them. Two different people were here at some point, this she knows for a fact.

INT. WASTELAND-HALF BURNED HOUSE

Shay hears movement above her. The noise was barely audible, but to her keen ears it was as loud as a fire engine's siren.

She cautiously walks up the stairs making sure to walk near the space where the step meets the wall, so the rotted wood won't creek under her step. Stopping when she spots a hidden door in the ceiling, leading to the attic, she notices that a minor amount of dust has been displaced. It's times like these that she hates being short. Slowly she moves a small brass table directly under the ceiling door and silently crawls atop it.

INT. WASTELAND-HALF BURNED HOUSE-ATTIC

Shay pokes her head through the small opening. She spots Frost and an older woman at the opposite corner. The two ladies slide on the last of their clothes and secure their weapons in their sheaths.

SHAY

"Frost!"

Frost and the woman jump in surprise. They turn toward the voice to see the vibrant hair and focused eyes of Shay. Being too short to clear the small opening, Shay props her feet against the wall to take some of the weight off of her arms.

SHAY CONT'D

Cocking her head toward the strange woman:

"Who are you?"

RAYNE

"Rayne. What's up?"

Shay nods then lowers herself down and plants her feet back on the table top. The others follow shortly.

EXT. WASTELAND

The three ladies make their way through the destroyed city ducking and skirting between cover points. They bypass clusters of the once human husks that roam the streets in mobs. These particular creatures usually sleep during the day and hunt at night. The fact that these withered things were out in the open with the sun shining bright was unnerving. The ladies keep their heads on a constant swivel, taking in all the information they can, and only moving when they were sure that the coast was clear.

FROST

"I know my father didn't send you all the way out here just to find me, so what the hell are you doing?"

Shay knows that Frost is completely capable of taking care of herself, but she also knows that even the most skilled soldiers can be overwhelmed by a pack of determined beasts.

SHAY

"I'm trying to help you avoid a painful end."

RAYNE

"This place isn't that bad."

Shay lifts her sleeve and checks the chrono strapped to her wrist. She knits her eyebrows as she worries about what little time they have to get to Mecca. She knows that when those bombs drop anything within the blast radius will have their atoms ripped apart. She looks in the direction of their end

---

destination.

SHAY

"Well no, but it will be once the tribes meet and set off the bombs."

RAYNE

"What bombs? I thought all the weapons were destroyed or used in the beginning."

SHAY

"Nope. A few of our scouts had found a cache of weapons stashed at an old military base."

FROST

"So the plan is to destroy everything and hope we get them as well? That sounds like a human thing to do."

Shay knows where Frost stands on this particular topic and knows that it has truly become their only option.

SHAY

Annoyed and impatient:

"It's worth a shot."

Frost shakes her head in disgust. The ladies walk in silence to avoid a confrontation in the open. After a few hours they come to the mouth of the cave Shay and Frost had called home. Outside, littering the entrance, they find bodies lying mangled and rotting.

RAYNE

"Oh no."

Frost runs inside the cave in a panic. Rayne calls after her but is ignored. Frost had only been gone a day. All the bodies belong to the adults and it pains Frost to know that all the children are gone. All the people she knew and cared for are now dead. A torrent of raw emotions flood her senses and causes a dull but painful ache in her chest.

INT. SUB. CAVE

The bodies of her people lay in pieces all over the caverns. The ground is soaked with blood and the smell of death fills the cave making the air foul and difficult to breath.

Stepping over rigid bodies to get to the living quarters, Frost fears the worst. Frost heads towards her father's room only to find him face down on the ground dead. A dark pool of still drying blood encloses him in a crimson halo.

INT. SUB. CAVE-KAIDEN'S ROOM

Frost stumbles over to her father and turns his stiffening body over. The dead man's muscles and tendons that are now deep in the stages of rigor mortis crack with every movement. The hole in his chest is deep. The blood is still a little moist due to the damp air. She holds him close, but no tears roll down her cheeks and this surprises her. The grief is there but that is it. It's just present in her chest.

Sengi steps out of the darkness. Her dark metal heeled boots make a tapping sound against the rock that Frost can barely hear in her grief and shock.

SENGI

"I've been looking all over for you."

The voice chills the grieving girl to her marrow. Slowly Frost looks up to see her mother standing a few meters from her. Her eyes fill with warm salty water. There is a part of her that is jumping for joy and another that is screaming in outrage and terror.

FROST

"Mom?"

SENGI

"Now be a good little girl for mommy and come here."

Caught in the absolute shock of seeing her mother after so many years sends Frost over the edge and the tears flow uncontrollably. Frost gently places her father's body back on the ground. She begins to rise to embrace her mother, but is quickly knocked back down with such force that her spine and head bounce off the solid stone. Gasping for air, Frost attempts to pick herself up off the ground, but then the dim lights of the room are replaced by a bright flash that fills her vision. The

E.A. Rodriguez

pain that followed nearly caused her to black out.

Sengi kicks Frost in the head again causing her to see actual stars. Frost falls to the ground and crawls away on pure instinct. Her eyes flutter violently as she fights to hold on to consciousness. The survival instinct takes over injecting Frost's blood with adrenaline. She jumps to her feet still in shock but ready. Tears fall from her eyes, but her vision is surprisingly clear.

FROST

"Mom stop!"

In a flash of movement, Sengi grabs Frost by the neck and pushes her against the wall knocking the wind from the young warrior's lungs. The strength of her mother is astounding. Frost fights back with little effect. Struggling to find an opening, Frost finally and reluctantly begins to strike her mother. Alarms are going off in her head as the oxygen in her lungs and blood is expended in the struggle.

FROST CONT'D

Gasping for air:

"Mom, Please!"

Frost strikes the bend of Sengi's elbow causing her grip to loosen. Frost takes the opening to knee lift Sengi in the gut causing her to release her grip completely. Sengi staggers back, then extends her arm out to her side and in an instant a sword rips the flesh of her palm. The bone sword flies out, Sengi takes hold of it and lunges at Frost. Dodging the initial attack Frost pleads with her mother. When that doesn't work Frost runs out into the main hall making sure to not step on or trip over the corpses littering the cold ground.

INT. SUB. CAVE-MAIN ROOM

Frost turns quickly toward her mother and fires an energy ball that pushes Sengi back into a wall, knocking a few rocks above loose. With catlike reflexes, Sengi rises to her feet and leaps at her daughter slashing. Frost successfully dodges her mother's attacks. Slash after slash she looks on, puzzled to see her mother attacking her in an almost frantic state. For a moment Frost thought that she had seen tears building in her mother's eyes.

FROST

"Mother, please stop!"

Sengi manages to slice the upper arm of her daughter. Hot blood spurts from the wound. Frost jumps back to get away from her murderous mother. She narrowly escapes another slash and clenches the wound on her arm as the warmth runs down her limb then drips from her fingers. Frost knows the cut is deep and may need to be stitched up. The wound stings but there isn't a whole lot that can be done about it at the moment. Sengi runs at her wounded daughter, sword trailing behind her and then in one fluid motion, Sengi drops down and slides over to Frost catching her off guard. Sengi fires a massive energy blast.

Frost tries to move out the way, but gets clipped on the side of her abdomen. The ball of energy and Frost is vaulted toward the ceiling where it explodes, causing the roof of the cave to blow apart. Frost had barely enough time to encase herself in a protective bubble before the ball erupted. Tons of rock, dirt and a single human are ejected into the sky.

EXT. WASTELAND-OUTSIDE THE CAVE

Frost is sent flying through the air along with the shattered rocks. Rayne and Shay look on surprised.

Frost crashes to the ground and immediately guards herself against the debris. The rocks and boulders rain down around her. Sengi leaps out of the giant hole to continue the attack.

Frost stumbles to her feet and is caught in a blitz of lightning fast strikes from Sengi. The rapid series of kicks, punches and elbow strikes follow one another in a staccato rhythm. Each blow devastates Frost until a kick to her upper thigh causes her to lose her balance. Seeing the opening, Sengi lands a spinning upward round house kick to the face of Frost and she is sent flying through the air again. Frost knows that she can't stay on the defensive or she will surely be killed by this thing that looks like her mother.

Frost pulls out two chained daggers from the pouch on her hip and throws them at Sengi while still in the apex of her flight. Each dagger pierces the chest of the woman and comes to a stop when they are embedded into the ground behind her. Slowly, the possessed mother takes hold of the chains.

Once on solid ground, Frost sends an electric shock through the chains, sending her mother's body into violent convulsions. Teeth gritted, muscles locked up tight, Sengi tries with all her will power to pull the chains free of her body and after a moment she collapses. Sengi screams in pain as the volts course through her body.

Frost stops the assault. The deluge of tears shows no sign of slowing. Her body feels week, her heart that had been seized by the icy grip of pain and anger melts away taking with it huge chunks of her soul, leaving a shattered, scared wreck.

Sengi (Fionala) quivers for a few moments before she climbs to her knees and takes an appreciative look at her daughter. The smile that stretches across her face is bitter sweet. The tears that had been locked in her eyes fall freely.

SENGI (FIONALA)

"You've grown up to be the strong woman I've always known you'd be, baby girl."

FROST

"Mom!"

Frost runs over to her mother and holds her. She looks down at the bloody chains in her mother's chest. Indecision, fear and all kinds of hurt grip the young woman. Looking at her mother in this state is far worse than the memory of seeing the crowd of monsters around her.

FROST CONT'D

"Mom, I'm so sorry."

Sengi (Fionala) looks at her daughter and caresses her face. Her red rimmed eyes cry tears of blood that runs down her cheeks. Lacking the strength to speak, Fionala mouths the words, "I love you." Before she smiles at her daughter one last time. All first aid training has completely escaped the normally collected mind of Frost as she shakes her mother in a childlike attempt to wake her from a deep sleep.

FROST

"MOM! Mom! No! Mom!"

CHAPTER 8

INT. DARK FORTRESS

Belial watches as his troops are being prepared to head out for battle. By the hundreds of thousands they grab their weapons of choice and fit themselves with armor. The fires of the forge flicker throughout the large room and reach the balconies where Belial and Izeta stand watching their Legions prepare.

The red glow of the fires down below act as a sort of battle paint as the glow dances on faces of the two high demons.

IZETA

"The minions are anxious, my Lord. They can't wait to be rid of the last humans in this region. It truly is a shame we cannot live in peace with them."

Belial clenches his jaw shut while he watches muscle bound demons pull sizable horned beasts out of pens and place saddles on them. The coats of these cat-like creatures are a mottled grey on black, with a shimmering exoskeleton guarding the ribs and spine. *Other lesser demons order the others into formation. One by one the demons fall into line and await the order of their respective generals. Belial looks down at his mechanical arm. Cold fury burns in his eyes.*

BELIAL

"Head out to where the animals plan to make their last stand. Destroy all of them and if you happen to sniff out anyone from Michael's bloodline, bring them to me so I can take care of them properly."

IZETA

Smiling:

"With pleasure my Lord."

Izeta fades into the darkness. His younger brother, Belial remains on the balcony to watch his men. The King of Demons watches his warriors swarm into formation. An evil smile creeps across his face.

EXT. SUB. CAVE-WASTELAND

Frost walks up to the mound where she has buried her mother and plants a wooden makeshift cross deep in the ground. Shay and Rayne watch in grim silence as Frost clinches the dirt in her fist and cries. Frost feels what little is left of her soul turn brittle then crumble away and carried on the winds as the storm builds in the sky overhead.

The clouds swell into a thick darkness. The winds gain strength and blow walls of dust through the air. Off in the distance lightning strikes the Earth. The crackling echo of the strike fills the void of silence. After a few moments have passed and the freezing rain begins to fall, Frost stands and looks down at the grave. Her eyes filled with pain and anger, she turns to walk away. Shay attempts to go up to her grieving friend to comfort her but is stopped by Rayne.

RAYNE

Holding Shays shoulder:

"Give her some time. There isn't a thing you can say to make her feel any better right now."

Shay looks back at the older lady, anger and hurt flickering in her eyes as well as her voice.

SHAY

"She shouldn't be alone right now."

RAYNE

"You're probably right, but in order for her to feel some sort of peace, she's going to need that anger to get her through. She's either gonna let it destroy her or use it as a tool. It's her choice at this point. Don't take that away from her."

Shay turns and looks at Frost with sympathy. Watching her friend walk off reminds her of her own losses past and recent. It numbs her chest to the point where she can hardly feel her own heartbeat.

Frost continues to walk. Her eyes are focused on the horizon in the distance. Thousands of thoughts and memories race through her mind. She remembers mixing chocolate pudding with her mother in the kitchen. They made such a mess, but they didn't care. The smile on her mother's face when it was covered in brown sweet goo was priceless. Frost blocks out the memories.

FROST

"You coming?"

Frost marches into the wastelands. Her tattered shroud dances in the wind of the bellowing storm.

RAYNE

"Let's go darlin'."

Shay and Rayne move to catch up to Frost. They follow Frost through the wasteland as they make their way to Mecca.

EXT. DARK FORTRESS

Solomn sits perched like a gargoyle on top of the castle. The clouds roll violently through the sky as the army moves out. He can't help but think how they all look like a growing disease that is spreading across this world, killing it with every step. He removes his mask to wipe away his frustrated tears. Feeling defeated, he looks toward the sky.

The thick iron door that leads to Solomn's perch creeks as it is carefully pushed opened. Belial stands in the doorway reading his son's hidden language. He feels the growing strife and perceives it as weakness. After a short moment, Belial makes his way to where Solomn sits.

BELIAL

"What troubles you my son?"

Solomn places the black and silver mask back over his face to hide his tears then rises to his feet to address his father.

SOLOMN

"Father, I told that man that his life would be spared. He posed no threat to us. He did not need to die."

The King narrows his eyes at his son's remarks. Keeping the disgust he feels from showing in his expression was no easy task for Belial.

BELIAL

"My son, this is war…"

Solomn grows tired of hearing the same excuse as to why good innocent people have to die. He can't bear to witness another child thrown in to slavery or added to the flesh pots. Before Belial is allowed to finish his rehearsed speech Solomn cuts him off in anger and frustration.

SOLOMN

"Why is there even a war to begin with? These people

fight with everything they've got just to live and we hunt them down like animals. Why?"

BELIAL

Annoyed:

"If it were up to these people they would have every single one of us wiped off the face of this mud-ball! Leaving us crippled without the decency of a quick and honorable death!"

The young Prince flinches at his father's sudden outburst. His head drops as he pretends to understand his father's reasoning. Belial heads inside the castle frustrated at his son's weakness for humanity.

SOLOMN

"My mother told me that this was once their world and we came to conquer it. Is it true that we started this war?"

The King stops just before the entrance of the castle. His anger almost crests at the mere mention of the failed experiment that was Fionala. He takes a few breaths before answering his son's foolish question. He looks at his cybernetic hand that rests on the door frame.

BELIAL

"This war was being waged long before Sengi was ever born. These animals had their chance at peace and they chose this path of death."

Belial moves to take a step but Solomn speaks again. It's like the boy is testing his patience.

SOLOMN

"Where is mother? I haven't seen her for a few days."

Belial's head turns slightly as he addresses his son. He speaks softly as not to alarm the boy.

BELIAL

"I sent, Sengi on a mission."

Confusion dominates Solomn's tone. The young Prince is not a fool. He knows that there is something amiss and that his father, along with a few others had been plotting against his mother. Some Lords didn't like having to treat a human as an equal.

SOLOMN

"But mother is not a soldier?!"

Seeing no need to say anymore, Belial walks inside the castle. Solomn balls his hands into tight fists. His short but razor sharp talons cut deep into his palms. He looks back out over the landscape to see the embodiment of death and destruction that his father once called "An army for salvation" ride further into the wasteland.

EXT. WASTELAND

Days have passed and the heat of the sun has sucked all the moisture from the ground leaving the land withered. The dust of the world is kicked up into the air as Isis and Izeta ride the four legged catlike beasts dubbed "The Cerberus."

The Legion, consisting of transformed humans, turned into dreadful monsters by the manticore parasites, monstrous demons riding equally terrifying beasts, followed by lesser foot soldiers.

The High Lords, charge full speed toward their prey until they spot something of interest. The ruins of Frost's former home can be seen in the distance. The collapsed pile of rocks draws the hordes attention. They keep riding through and they spot a single marked grave that peaks their curiosity.

Isis dismounts her ride, walks over to the solitary grave and kicks off the cross that was placed on top of it.

Izeta signals for a squad to search the cave and kill anyone inside then report back. Izeta knows that the extermination crew won't find anyone inside, but he thought it would be best to at least look as if they were working hard. He was more interested to see who was beneath the mound of dirt. Isis kneels down to trace a path in the dirt with her finger. She, like her brother has a pretty good idea who had been buried here.

ISIS

"This one must've been highly regarded. Let's take a peek."

Isis waves over a low ranked demon to dig up the grave. The short lanky creature jogs over. His long ears bob up and down with every long stride. He stops in front of Isis, panting like a dog in the heat.

INCUBUS

"Yes, my lovezly?"

Isis walks back over to her mount, caresses it's armored face and without turning back to the small wretched creature she speaks.

ISIS

"Dig!"

The dirty, almost mindless thing bounces up and down at the sound of her voice. He claps his hands together, bends over and begins to paw at the soil.

INCUBUS

"Yes, arousing one."

The Incubus scrapes his hands furiously in the dirt. After a few short moments the thing reveals the boots of Sengi. Izeta leans forward in curiosity.

The Incubus continues and moves to reveal the pale face of Sengi as she lay dead in the ground. The dirt that clings to her face does little to mar her beauty and the peaceful expression that make her features glow.

E.A. Rodriguez
ISIS

"So, there are survivors."

Izeta smiles at the statement. Anyone who could actively fight back against the magic of Belial was impressive indeed. So, it was only natural that their children would be as well. He couldn't wait to meet her daughter face to face and test her skill.

IZETA

"Yes. That much is clear, but whoever chose to bury Sengi must have known her in her former life. Which begs the question; is it the father or the daughter?"

The Incubus dances around Sengi's body with excitement. The thing can't help but be aroused at the sight of her. Izeta pinches the bridge of his nose to keep from splitting the nasty creature in two.

ISIS

"The husband is probably too old to have done this and besides he isn't the offspring of the ancient warrior mage Michael."

IZETA

"That only leaves the daughter. You know what the orders are when it comes to this particular matter."

Panting, the foul demon interrupts the siblings. He tries desperately to hide his erection.

INCUBUS

"Can I fuck this meats, my Lordz? It's so..."

With lightning speed, Izeta draws his sword and stops his swing so that the blade rests between the eyes of the small creature. The foul beast didn't even realize it was in danger until the general was shouting at him. The amount of venom in the High Lord's voice causes the creature shrink into himself.

IZETA

"If you so much as touch her, I will slowly castrate your sorry ass. Now fall back in line you depraved, vile piece of shit!"

The Incubus walks with haste back into formation like a dog with its tail between its legs. Isis giggles as the small thing runs away. Izeta just shoots her an impatient look.

ISIS

"We don't know if those two are still alive."

IZETA

"In any case this must be reported to Lord Belial."

The squad that had been sent to search the cave returns to Izeta with their report.

DEMON KNIGHT

"There is no sign of life inside, my Lord."

IZETA

"Good."

He scratches away at a piece of parchment in quick precise motions with his stylus and when he is satisfied that the message is clear he hands off the note to a messenger.

IZETA CONT'D

"Send a messenger back to the castle with this information."

The horned beast salutes.

DEMON KNIGHT

"My Lord."

ISIS

"So was there a reason Belial sent this woman to her death?"

IZETA

"The enchantment was starting to fade and Lord Belial got the son he wanted. The blood of Lailoken and that warrior flows through the veins of the Halfling. Her task was done and she was living on borrowed time. She was never intended for battle, this Belial knew."

Izeta sighs heavily. He liked the woman. She was strong and honorable. She was too fair a lady for his brother.

ISIS

Incredulous:

"So he knew she would be killed?"

IZETA

"Yes, but so did she. Why would she have thrown her life away willingly?"

ISIS

"Maybe she wanted to see her daughter one last time."

IZETA

"That is very possible."

Brows furrowed in analytical thought and respect for the human dubbed Sengi, the older demon elf can't help but feel sorry for the woman and her spawn. The emotion is quickly squashed as he looks back at the Legion behind him.

IZETA CONT'D

"Move out!"

The Legion is on the move again and the lone messenger moves in the opposite direction. The army walks past the grave and every single eye of every creature steals a glance at the fallen human who they all had come to respect over the years.

The Incubus that dug her up walks up over the grave. He looks to see if the generals are out of sight then reaches down and squeezes the dead woman's breasts, giggles, then scampers off to rejoin the countless others.

CHAPTER 9

EXT. WASTELAND-OLD WAREHOUSE

The dust storm builds momentum on the horizon enveloping whole city blocks in its abrasive embrace. An old storage house that was once used to store agricultural equipment stands strong against the coming storm. The trio identifies it as a stable structure to wait out the storm and head in its direction. The three ladies check the old warehouse for safety making sure that there are no immediate threats and head inside to avoid the storm.

INT. RUNDOWN WAREHOUSE

The old building is littered with trash. The once big powerful machines lay stripped of any valuable components. Scavenged for parts the machines have long since succumbed to the ravages of the elements. The second level is open to the rest of the floor plan. The walls show evidence of a fire from years past. The catwalk that stretches from end to end of the wide building looks as if it couldn't hold itself up against a strong gust of wind, but all the other platforms look sturdy enough to hide or defend, if it came to that.

RAYNE

"This place looks good to rest for awhile."

Shay sits on an old box and watches Frost walk up to the second level to be alone.

SHAY

"Do you think that she'll be alright?"

RAYNE

"How would you be dealing if everything you've known was gone and you had to kill your own mother?"

Shay's head hangs low as she thinks about what happened to her parents and the events of recent weeks. She quickly squashes any thought of William. There will hopefully be time to mourn his death later. Rayne peeks out the grime crusted windows to ensure that they have not been followed by any of the creatures that lurk in the wastelands.

INT. RUNDOWN WAREHOUSE-SECOND FLOOR

Frost walks to the far end of the open room and looks out the window. The dust storm headed their way can be seen moving with great speed as it whirls around the old city. Frost slowly kneels down and allows herself to cry. Her tears soak the layer of dirt on the rusted metal floor.

INT. DARK FORTRESS-MAP ROOM

The room is silent with only the massive fire place providing light as Belial sits in an ornate chair gazing into the flames. The demon messenger sprints through the halls, bypassing human servants as they toil about their duties. None of the humans dare to make eye contact with the speeding creature.

The demon comes to a halt just outside the room where Belial rests contemplating the steps he must take to ensure the complete irradiation of mankind, and the survival of his species. The demon knocks three times then waits. Once he is given permission to enter, he does with great speed.

DEMON

Kneeling in front of Belial:

"My Lord, I bring a message from Izeta and Isis."

The demon extends his arm holding the tiny scroll. Belial takes the rolled up paper and opens it to read its contents. When he is done reading the tight script he throws the parchment in fire and smiles.

BELIAL

"I knew that would draw her out."

INT. DARK FORTRESS-RAFTERS OF MAP ROOM

Solomn hides in the shadows of the rafters, watching his father converse with the messenger demon. He leans in as much as he can without completely falling over or giving away his position.

SOLOMN

"What is he talking about?"

INT. RUNDOWN WAREHOUSE

The storm rages on outside the walls of the warehouse while Shay and Rayne clean an area they have chosen as a suitable place to lay their heads for the night. Frost walks down from the second floor and joins her friends. Rayne taps on the floor next to her.

RAYNE

"Come on chick, cop a squat."

Frost sits down next to Rayne and rests her head on her shoulders. She wipes a stray tear from her face. Shay looks at Frost.

SHAY

"You ok?"

Frost nods her head which causes another tear to escape her eyes and roll down her check. Rayne reaches in a pouch and pulls out some dried meat and hands it to Frost.

RAYNE

"Here, eat some jerky. It'll make you feel better."

Frost takes the meat and examines it. It looks like dried deer but she knows that it's not.

FROST

"Is this that demon meat you were talking about? How can you eat this shit?"

RAYNE

"Take a bite and then you'll know."

SHAY

"Can I have some?"

Rayne tosses some jerky to Shay while Frost debates on whether she should eat it or not. Shay rips in to her piece of dried monster meat like a starving child.

SHAY CONT'D

"Oh my God this is good! Frost you have got to try it."

Frost looks at Shay unsure and takes a small bite. After a couple of seconds of chewing, Frost devours the jerky.

Outside, the storm has come and gone. The sun begins to fade away in hues of pinks and violets. Frost sleeps silently while Rayne and Shay talk.

E.A. Rodriguez
RAYNE

"I've always heard rumors during the war that the demons were looking for certain people with some special lineage. I didn't think it was true."

SHAY

"Frost and I grew up together. She told me about this dream she has often. It's more of a memory really. When the monsters came through the hyper gate and started killing everyone. She always thought her mother had been killed, but she felt her every day."

Looking down at the sleeping lady, Rayne can't help but feel sorry for her. She couldn't imagine having to kill her own parents.

RAYNE

"Well that wasn't the case now was it? Why did they take her? That's the million dollar question."

SHAY

"Well, the enemy's actions kinda confirmed the suspicions of a special bloodline. Certain people were and are still targeted and taken away. Upon further investigation a link was found."

Rayne leans in. Her brows furrowed and her eyes beg Shay to continue the explanation. Rayne had heard the rumors, but nothing ever came of them. She knew that certain groups of people were taken away but she, like others, thought those unfortunate souls were taken to the flesh pots.

FROST

Eyes still closed:

"I'm asleep not dead. Keep it down."

The two ladies look at each other, laugh, and try to ease the mood.

RAYNE

Sarcastic tone:

"Sorry Frosty, we didn't know that you needed your beauty sleep that much. We'll keep things to a whispa' from here on out."

SHAY

Laughing:

"Sorry Frost..."

Rayne get's up from her seat on the floor, walks over to the giant bay window and looks out. She can see the dust blown landscape and it is almost like the state of nature reflects the chaotic state of every person still alive. The world is still beautiful, from a distance, but if you get too close you can see all scars that mar this garden.

Shay leans over toward Frost from her seated position using her elbow to prop herself up.

SHAY CONT'D

"Hey girl. You alright?"

FROST

"I just need some time."

Frost closes her eyes. She had heard the tales regarding the bloodlines but had always dismissed them as pure fantasy. Why or how could her family be so special? After seeing her mother again gave some credence to the old stories. This she could not deny. Shay leans back over to her original position, sits up right and looks at Rayne with a sympathetic glance. She thought that she could see a thin sheen roll down Rayne's cheek and glint in the sunlight. Shay watches as Rayne wipes away the lone tear. With that single motion, Shay realizes that every single person is adrift and trying to find their way in this scarred hell. They have all lost a great deal in this new world and if man's last stand doesn't go as planned, they will lose what's left.

CHAPTER 10

EXT. WASTELAND

The sun rises above the scorched earth. The morning winds blow, and the dust flows through the air as it whips around the broken buildings. The Legion makes its way through the once stunning mega city. The grunting and howling of the beasts echo through the empty shell that was once a bustling metropolis.

INT.RUNDOWN WAREHOUSE

The women wake up in a state of shock. They quickly gather their things and peek out the windows to see a dust trail in the distance. They know they must get moving or face certain death.

FROST

"Shit!"

Rayne can feel her heart sinking as the massive dust cloud drifts into the air. The loud thumping of her heart almost drowns out any noises of the outside world.

RAYNE

"How many do you think are out there?"

Frost slowly shakes her head. She closes her mouth to swallow but it's dry.

FROST

"Too many."

Shay runs over and looks out the window, mouth a gape. Frost runs over to their pile of supplies and gathers them up as quickly as possible.

FROST

"We have to get the fuck out of dodge before those things get here."

Shay rips her gaze from the window, runs over to her pack and straps it to her back.

SHAY

"Their speed doesn't leave us a lot of time."

RAYNE

"Then we better get moving."

The trio make their way out of the building and run ahead of the marching soldiers. They stay parallel to the Legion so that they might pass them up, reach a point where they can sneak away, and with any luck not get spotted or sniffed out by the manticores.

Frost leans over and whispers to Shay.

FROST

"Why the hell are there so many?"

Shay cups her mouth with her hands to make sure that not a sound travels to enemy ears.

SHAY

"Could they have found out?"

In a narrow ally, Rayne guards the rear making sure that they will not be flanked. The pounding of many boots begins to sound like thunder as the monstrous force draws closer.

FROST

"What? You think they found out about that last ditch effort to try and kill them? That's a possibility. I mean, that's no ordinary death squad. That's a mobile cluster fuck heading for our last hope."

Rayne signals to Frost and Shay. She points up to an old fire escape to get a better view.

She jumps up to grab a hold of the metal wreck and makes her way on to the roof. To the surprise of the ladies the rusted metal ladder is sturdy and doesn't make a sound. Shay and Frost follow closely behind trying to make as little noise as possible.

EXT. WASTELAND-ROOFTOP

The trio crawls to the edge of the building and look out toward the massive horde of demons.

RAYNE

"Holy hell! That's a lot of soldiers."

FROST

"Well they aren't out on a morning jog. Something big is going down."

SHAY

"The only thing that is going down is the unification of the clans. All that's left of us will be wiped out if we don't get a message out to them."

RAYNE

"Well there isn't much that we could do right now. We can't send word of this, and there isn't a point in all of us dying trying to fight all those things."

SHAY

"So what are you saying? We just let them go on their way and kill everyone in this region? You're fucking crazy."

Frost catches her friend's green eyes. The intensity in both their eyes was enough to rip apart some unfortunate soul's heart. Both ladies would not back down, but Frost had checked her emotions when she buried her mother while, Shay was still feeling the pain of loss from nineteen years ago.

FROST

"It blows, Shay but that's the only thing we can do at this point."

The horde passes right under the building the three women occupy. The choking smell of dead flesh from the manticores is thick in the air around them causing their eyes to water for a moment. The girls lay flat on their backs hoping not to be discovered by the angry mob of demons that are on the march directly below them.

SHAY

"We should at least try and beat them to the base and give the others a heads up rather than let them get caught with their pants around their ankles."

RAYNE

"I was thinking of something similar. It's worth a shot. I've got an idea."

FROST

"It'll be hard, but it is worth a shot. Let's move."

The three ladies peer over the side of the building to see if there is an opening, so that they may get a move on, but the vast numbers of the horde doesn't seem to be letting up. The trio sneaks over to an area where their foes are loosely packed and

make their way across the rooftops, around the two Legions.
They run ahead making sure to stay out of sight.

EXT. WASTELAND

The lone scout that was sent to report on the status of Sengi
makes his way back to the Legion. Solomn follows closely
behind the dutiful demon, shortening the distance with every
step he makes sure to stick to cover behind old vehicles and old
business high rises. The Prince patiently waits for the moment
to strike. The unsuspecting demon pauses for a moment to
evaluate the surrounding area, but that is all the time his tail
needed. Solomn runs up to the scout, grabs a hold of the
demon's armor, spins it around and pins him against an old
stone building. The creature's head smashes into the brick
building so hard that some horns on the back of its head are
crushed. Seeing who's got him in a tight grip the demon
becomes outraged.

DEMON

"What is the meaning of this?"

SOLOMN

"What did you report to my father, demon?"

The messenger holds his tongue in defiance. His has little
respect for those who are not full blood. The Prince's patience
for sycophants had been wearing thin over the past few days
and there wasn't time to for a lengthy interrogation. Solomn
takes a hold of the dark thing's upper arm firmly and with a

265

quick yank the demon's arm is separated from its body.

SOLOMN CONT'D

"Answer me!"

A fountain of dark viscous ichor spills out from the hole where the demons arm once rested. The demon screams in agony. Face torn in a rictus of pain the demon still refuses to answer the half-breed Prince.

SOLOMN CONT'D

"You can answer me or I will rip off every single limb and slice apart your organs one tiny sliver at a time."

The demon spits in the Prince's face. Luckily he was wearing his mask. In response, Solomn produces a long slender blade and firmly presses its point in a gap of the ugly creature's armor near the groin. A silent question burns to be answered in the eyes of the Prince.

DEMON

"You weren't supposed to know."

SOLOMN

"Know what?"

The demon shakes his head from side to side, obviously debating the merits of answering his captor's questions.

DEMON

"Your mother. She was sent on a mission that was to be the death of her. Your father had one last task for her before she outlived her usefulness."

SOLOMN

"What was her mission?"

DEMON

"I can't..."

Solomn jabs the thin blade past the leather gap and into flesh. He twists with quick precise motions. The demon cries out in pain.

DEMON CONT'D

"She, she was sent out to locate her daughter. It was a mission Lord Belial knew she would not survive. He wants the daughter!"

The Prince breath becomes heavy as he is flooded with a torrent of emotions from the realization that his mother just might be gone. At the same time a strange hope that he might be able to find a sister that he never knew existed gives him focus. The moment is interrupted when the foul creature in his grasp opens its mouth.

DEMON

"I have told you all that I know, release me half breed."

Solomn holds the demon a bit longer while he processes what he has just learned. The savage smile that cracks the Prince's face goes unnoticed by the scout, but if he had noticed it, he would have known what was about to come.

SOLOMN

"I will release you demon."

The young half blood's eyes glow a bright red. The vermillion hue illuminates his angelic features that are always hidden under his mask.

SOLOMN CONT'D

"I will release you in to the underworld, where your pathetic soul will be devoured for all eternity!"

The demon tries to break free, but his attempts are quickly squashed when Solomn puts his fist through the demons head. Its head instantly explodes, showering the wall and part of the street. Covered with chunks of skull, teeth and brain matter, Solomn let's go of the headless body. He looks at his shaking bloody hand in shock at what he just done.

The Prince of the Dökkálfar looks up at the sky for a moment and breathes deeply in an attempt to calm his nerves. Then he takes off sprinting in the direction of the Legions. His Mind races with thoughts that he doesn't have the time to process. Even if he found his mother alive what would he say? Hell. What would he say if he found his sister? He couldn't think of anything witty at the moment, but he hoped that he would at least have the chance to greet her before she tried to kill him.

CHAPTER 11

EXT. WASTELAND-RUINED CITY

Frost, Rayne and Shay move as fast as they can to beat the thousands of demons to their destination, but they can see that even though they are running at top speed the Legions are not that far behind them. Frost slows to a jog before stopping. Resting her hands on her knees for support, Frost peers over her shoulders at the tireless mass of creatures.

FROST

"We'll never get far enough ahead of them at this rate!"

SHAY

"You're right. We'll have to rest at some point."

Frost and Shay look at the horror that is headed their way. Hope slowly fading from their eyes as they breathe heavily and the grim reality begins to set in.

FROST

"We need some way to slow them down."

Rayne looks at the approaching mob and looks at the ground in deep thought. Probably arguing with herself.

RAYNE

"Well, there ain't any way around this one. You ladies are just gonna have to go on without me."

SHAY

"Could you repeat that? I had something bat shit crazy in my ear."

The expression is one of total shock. Shay cannot believe what she just heard. Understanding washes over Frost then she moves closer to Rayne. Rayne shakes her head no. Frost pauses half a meter away.

FROST

"There has to be another way to do this Rayne."

Frost takes Rayne by the arm and pulls her gently around to face her. Both of their eyes are glassy with warm tears. Rayne pulls Frost into a fierce embrace. She swallows to keep her voice from cracking.

RAYNE

"We don't have time to sit here and braid each other's hair."

SHAY

"Rayne you can't do this. I know you're tough but there

are just too many of those things! You can't!"

Rayne turns to look down the hill at the growing dust trail. She takes a deep calming breath and relaxes her muscles.

RAYNE

"You have got to go now. I will buy you the time you need to get things done. I will meet up with you two later. Now go on!"

Rayne hugs Frost and Shay one more time then pushes them away. She turns to face the oncoming Legions. Breathing deeply as a result of the adrenaline coursing through her veins, Rayne smiles with true resolve in her mind and begins to form a battle plan. She knows that battle plans are only good for the first few moments. She also knows that it's better to have one or ten when shit really hits the fan than to have none.

FROST

"You better make it out of this alive."

With her back to the ladies, Rayne raises her open left hand as if to say goodbye and waits.

Frost takes hold of Shay's arm and pulls her away. They pump their sore legs harder trying to put some distance between them and their enemy. The previous exhaustion is forgotten. They use the pain of knowing that someone they have come to care for, though not for long, was about to risk everything to give them a chance. Looking back, Frost can see Rayne pulling her pack from her shoulders, setting it on the ground and rummaging through it. She pulls out a couple of tiny pouches and places them in the side pockets of her pack. Frost can see that the old war hero still has a few tricks up her sleeve. She only hopes that those tricks were good enough to keep her alive.

EXT. WASTELAND-RUINED CITY

Izeta raises his hand as he stops to make his soldiers halt. He squints trying to see what appears to be a lone human in the distance walking out from behind some buildings to his left.

IZETA

"Do you see that Isis?"

ISIS

Curiosity and smug contempt smothers her voice:

"What is she doing out here all by herself, I wonder?"

The old warrior suppresses a smile at the sight of a worthy advisory.

IZETA

"I think I've seen her before, but I can't remember where."

ISIS

"Well seeing as how the great Izeta is getting old, maybe I should handle this one."

Izeta smiles, then nods, and motions for his erstwhile sister to move forward. He thinks it'll be an amusing sight to see his sister try to remove the deceptively diminutive obstacle from their path. The truth was that the older brother had seen this small woman before. Nearly two decades ago, he witnessed her completely wipe out the Sky Dragon Company almost single handedly and with frightening ease. He hadn't seen her since that time, but he knew this one will not go down easily, so he was very willing to let, Isis "handle" it. Isis smiles and begins to move forward with her Legion of demons following closely behind her. The smile on her face reads of pure misguided bravado.

As Rayne waits patiently she notices that the sun is directly above her and can't help but think of an old western duel at high noon. She smiles at the thought.

ISIS

"It would appear that this human has a death wish! Let us grant it."

Rayne lifts her head at the sound of Isis speaking. A jolt of rage shoots down her spine causing her to shake with anticipation. Her fingers twitch as she waits for the perfect moment to launch her attack on the single minded fiends that follow the big breasted hussy.

RAYNE

"Bring it bitch."

Swinging her right arm forward in a cutting motion, Isis

signals for her troops to advance and overwhelm the lone human.

ISIS

"Kill the little pest."

The scores of demons charge at Rayne full speed. The spittle flows from their mouths at the thought of eating her alive.

Rayne pulls a tiny metal sphere, the size of a base-ball, from the side pocket of her pack. She presses a button then throws it straight up into the air.

The fierce beasts continue to run toward her snarling and grunting all the way. Rayne spins around and kicks the ball toward the horde of monsters. The metal ball hurdles through the air spinning. When it finally speeds past the first few lines of demons it violently explodes in a blinding white flash. The concussive force throws tiny ball bearings in every direction that pass through flesh and armor completely without losing momentum. At the same time the searing heat vaporizes those nearest to the epicenter of the blast. In an instant a couple hundred enemy troops are gone.

Rayne begins her attack running full speed towards the dismembered beasts that were destroyed in the blast. Reaching into the outer pockets of her pack, Rayne throws sticky sacks on the outer walls of every building as she passes them. She reaches inside the small pack on her back, pulls out two dull metal rods, and ignites them with a sizzling hiss to reveal military grade plasma daggers. Each dagger is about a foot and half long. They will cut through anything like a hot knife *through butter.*

The demons just outside the blast range try to pick themselves up, but they are too slow to react and are quickly knocked back down to their knees. Rayne blows through them. Mini Plasma blades in hand, Rayne slices through the bodies and limbs of the already battered beasts.

While swinging her weapons with deadly precision, Rayne reaches in her pouch for another grenade and throws it forward without missing a beat in her assault. Spinning and twirling her yellow blades of death at anything that moves. She ducks under what could have been a crippling blow and jams the super heated plasma in the groin of a bull-like creature. Then she jumps up and forward parting the beast right up the center, cauterizing the tissue while fusing any internal organs together. Rayne slices a manticore in two as she leaps forward in a twisting summersault and kicks the already airborne grenade into the charging mass of monsters.

EXT. WASTELAND-RUINED CITY

Frost and Shay run as fast as they can through the debris filled city. Leaping over destroyed cars and crumbling buildings. They hear another explosion where Rayne is fighting for her life.

SHAY

"We have to go back!"

Running:

"Going back now will be pointless. If she died and we went back, her death would have been for nothing."

Reluctantly, Shay turns and continues to follow Frost. Tears flow from her eyes as she thinks of Rayne and the horrors she is facing alone.

EXT. WASTELAND-RUINED CITY-BATTLE

The demons slowly and very cautiously close in around, Rayne as she stands on guard in the middle of the carnage plotting her next move. Rayne breathes heavily as she weighs her options.

Watching her soldiers get obliterated, by this small framed woman completely throws Isis into a rage. She cannot believe that one person is capable of so much destruction.

ISIS

Voice cracking in anger:

"It's just one woman you worthless maggots! Kill her!"

IZETA

"Are you having trouble little sister? Do you want me, the old man to end this for you?"

An icy rage spills over Isis. She jerks her head toward her older brother.

ISIS

"Back off! If you even try to interfere with this battle I will personally rip your balls off!"

With a sardonic smile Izeta just nods.

IZETA

"As you wish."

Isis kicks her Cerberus to charge into the battle. Her fury at being shown up by a human has blinded her so much that she tramples and crushes her own soldiers.

Rayne turns and braces for the attack. When she realizes that a huge snarling beast is headed her way, she throws a tomahawk. The curved metal blade slices through bone and embeds itself in the head of the Cerberus, killing it in mid stride. Isis leaps off her dead beast as it skids across the cracked and weed covered pavement. She lets loose a barrage of throwing knives at Rayne.

Anticipating the attack, Rayne jumps back and deflects all but one of the projectiles. The last knife finds a home in Rayne's upper thigh sending shocks of electricity racing through her nerves, causing her to wince in pain.

Rayne lands and tries to remove the dagger. There's no time. She has to defend herself from the attacks of the remaining demons. With her mobility severely hampered, Rayne knows that she has to end this and fast.

Rayne expertly dodges and delivers killing blows to each demon as they attack her. Rayne looks to see that Isis is sprinting in her direction to join the battle. A noise just behind Rayne distracts her for just a split second, but it was a critical second. Isis pulls back her fist and knocks the daylights out of Rayne while she was defending against another demon's attack. Rayne is pushed back, her feet slide along the ground before she comes to a stop. Still standing and prepares for the coming assault.

RAYNE

Wiping the blood from her lip:

"What the fuck was that? A love tap? If that's all you've got, you might as well turn around and take your sorry ass back the way you came."

Isis becomes enraged and charges Rayne. She strikes with a knee lift that Rayne tries to dodge, but with the dagger still protruding from her leg, she wasn't fast enough. Rayne gets clipped in the side of her ribcage and is knocked up in the air toward the building at her back. While Rayne tries to catch her breath, Isis charges in to finish her off. Right before Rayne hits the building she regains control and throws one of her plasma sabers at Isis stopping her in her tracks. The hot blade pierces the demon's shoulder. The She Demon shrieks in pain as the plasma burns her flesh and begins to slide down causing more damage.

Rayne smiles as she pulls the dagger out of her leg and runs towards the injured woman. The high demon pulls the plasma saber from her arm just as Rayne delivers a jumping knee lift to her face. As the demon recoils, Rayne comes down with the dagger and plunges it into the demon general's collar bone, shattering it and completely collapsing one of the lungs.

Rayne feels a burning sensation and looks down to see that Isis has stabbed her in the stomach with her own plasma dagger. The evil woman smiles and spits the blood that was filling her mouth into the face of her foe.

Seeing that there isn't much that Isis can do, Izeta sends his Legion to finish the battle as the two ladies have come to a draw. Rayne watches as the demons charge at them and laughs to herself.

RAYNE

"Hey! When you woke up this morning did you think that you would be dying like this? You cock juggling thunder cunt!"

Isis tries to talk, but can only muster enough strength to continue holding Rayne in place.

As the demons draw near, Rayne reaches down and pulls out a detonator switch. Isis tries to reach up to stop her, but catches a forehead to the nose instead. Rayne feels the cartilage snap and cave into the woman's face in a spray of black blood. Isis squeals. Once the demons are close enough, Rayne presses the button igniting the sticky bundles of C10 explosives she threw on the walls of the buildings at the start of the battle.

One by one the C10 explodes, bringing down the buildings

around them in a storm of dust, debris and gore.

EXT. WASTELAND-CLIFF SIDE

The massive explosions can be seen from the distance that the two ladies have put between them and the horde. The high rise buildings crumble to the ground and in the process colliding with the buildings that are in close range, dragging them down as well.

SHAY

"Do you think she made it out of that?"

FROST

"It's hard telling. If she's alive she will meet up with us at Mecca."

The dust cloud is so thick that it blocks out the sun as buildings continue to fall. Frost and Shay continue on their path.

CHAPTER 12

EXT. WASTELAND-DESTROYED CITY

Hours later, the dust has had time to settle on the battle ground. The landscape rests in a dense fog, which blots out most of the sun's rays, casting an eerie blue gray tint on the surrounding area. The thick dust makes it hard to see or even breathe. The sun hangs low in the sky. The bodies of dismembered demons litter the streets along with bent steel, crushed vehicles and huge chunks of stone.

Solomn runs through the carnage to find that a huge battle took place here. He moves some of the rubble and just finds severed body parts. He stands and begins to move in the direction Frost and Shay had escaped. He pauses when he spots a blood trail and follows it to the side of a crumbling building. He finds a bloody and badly wounded Isis. Hearing footsteps behind her, Isis rolls over on her back to see Solomn approaching her.

ISIS

"Solomn, what are you doing here? It doesn't matter. Help me."

Isis extends her good arm toward the Prince.

SOLOMN

"What do you know of this plot against my mother?"

The wounded general looks up at the Prince with such scorn and annoyance that he would even be asking her about what she thought of as a trivial matter. For a moment she wonders if she should scold him for his disrespect, but thinks better of it.

ISIS

"What does it matter? Your mother was a pawn. She was a dull tool. Now help me you half-blood pig."

Solomn slowly walks up to the injured Isis. He places his hand on her wounded shoulder causing Isis to howl in pain and helps her up. Once she is on her feet he shoves his thumb into the hole the plasma saber had made causing the vile woman to silently scream as she looks him in the eyes.

ISIS

"What are you doing you fool?"

He jams his thumb deeper inside the wound causing Isis to shriek in pain. With a cold unfeeling stare, he answers the woman. Isis notices his cold eyes and for the first time she fears the man standing before her. The fear coupled with the pain of her earlier battle causes the woman to tremble.

SOLOMN

"What does it look like I'm doing? I'm helping just as you asked."

Isis screams in agonizing pain as he uncaringly wiggles his thumb around until he finds bone and tightens his grip. Solomn takes hold of her other shoulder firmly. With his thumb already in the wound he uses it's placing in the injured arm as a starting point and begins to slowly rip off her arm. Isis screams again, but her cries are cut short when Solomn clamps down on her throat and squeezes. Her knees begin to buckle under the immense pain and stress. Isis nearly collapses, but only drops a few inches as Solomn tightens his hold on her.

SOLOMN

"My mother may have been just a pawn to you, but she was my world. She was my God! I will see to it that this planet is cleansed of every last one of you heartless wretches, even if it costs me my life to do so."

Isis struggles for air as Solomn crushes her wind pipe, completely breaking every bone in her neck. He shakes the dead Lord from his grasp then drops her lifeless body. He looks at the woman who had caused him so much pain as a child for a span of a few heartbeats then he calmly walks away to continue his journey.

INT. DARK FORTRESS-DINING HALL

Belial enjoys a meal of lamb and rice at the long table with subordinates and subjects, when another scout bursts through the doors to deliver a message.

DEMON SCOUT

"My Lord, I bring you a message from General Izeta."

Belial takes the scroll, opens it, and begins to read its contents. He is quickly angered by the report. He stands up and walks toward the window.

BELIAL

"Fetch my son."

FORTRESS GUARD

"My Lord. Solomn left some days ago."

BELIAL

"Why wasn't I informed of this?"

Belial shifts to take hold of the frightened guard.

FORTRESS GUARD

"We thought it was under your orders, my Lord."

With blinding speed he tears off the demon's head. The others at the table stand at the ready.

BELIAL

"Ignorant fools!"

He turns to his men at the table. The look in his eyes unnerve them, but they are ready to obey.

BELIAL

"Fetch me my armor and ready my army!"

The demons run out of the room in haste. In a short while they return with trusted servants. Each one of the servants carries armfuls of supplies. They begin to dress him for battle.

BELIAL

"Must I do everything myself?"

Belial's eyes glow with an evil mist as his armor is being placed on his body and the leather straps tightened. Once dressed and armored, Belial grabs his spear. He leaps through the window.

EXT. WASTELAND

Belial hits the ground running with super human speed and heads toward the location of the human base. The gates to the fortress open and Legions of demons rush out to support their master in the coming battle.

EXT. WASTELAND-OUTSKIRTS

Shay and Frost speed toward their destination that is finally in sight. The base looks deserted from a distance. The old military installation is overgrown with vines and trees that have found purchase at the base of the watchtowers. The Earth, it would seem, had taken the land back.

The two ladies make their way closer to the base. There appears to be no activity, but then spot lights shine down at them. The focused beams of light blinds the girls and stops them in mid step. A mechanically amplified voice rings out from unseen speakers.

OFFICER

"Stay right where you are or we will use deadly force."

The two ladies hold their hands up blinking away the shiny orbs that obscure their vision.

The gates open, a man with a squad of ten soldiers that are heavily armed and armored steps out. They make their way out to where the two ladies stand. Four guards in full exo-skeleton battle suits stand guard at the entrance. A bear of a man with a burn scarred face and eye patch over his left eye steps forward to address the duo. He is dressed in an old, but finely pressed uniform with many commendations pinned to his chest.

OZ

"I am Major General Oz and you must be Frost, Kaiden's daughter. We heard what had happened to your clan and we are sorry."

FROST

"What's with the muscle? Expecting trouble are we?"

"We had to make sure you two weren't infected with the Manticore."

Seeing that the ladies are indeed human, Oz turns and begins to walk back into the base. He motions for the ladies to follow him. Frost and Shay exchange a glance and begin to move.

OZ

"Come. We have much to get ready for."

The girls follow the Major General into the base. Shay looks at the towering mechanized armored suits with their .50 Caliber spinning guns mounted on their shoulders. The suits look like they've been through hell and back.

INT. MILITARY BASE

They make their way down into the old instillation and through a narrow corridor. The other soldiers from the many tribes stock pile ammunition and take food further down to the safe rooms located in the sublevels while the women and children who can't fight are led into a giant room that can be sealed by an equally giant blast door in those sublevels.

FROST

"The last time we encountered trouble there were at least two Legions of demons headed this way. One of our own stayed behind to buy us some time to warn you."

*Without missing a beat and presenting a professional calm, Oz
continues to stride down the corridor with Frost and Shay
following close behind.*

OZ

"We are well aware of the situation. We were informed
by one of our scouts about the approaching army and are
well equipped to deal with them."

*Frost's head cocks back as if she were physically hit by his
words. She quickens her pace so that she can walk side by side
the Major General.*

FROST

"You knew they were coming and your scouts didn't let
us know."

*The heated tone in Frost's voice shakes the calm from the man's
face, but only for a second. He grimaces slightly before putting
on his mask of calm control.*

OZ

"A scout's job is to gather intel that's all. We lost too
many who thought they'd be heroes in the beginning."

*Frost grabs the Major General by the shoulder, swinging him
around and plants a solid right hook, in his jaw knocking him
on his ass. She leans over him ready to follow up on a well
deserved ass beating. The men and women in the large passage
stop what they are doing to watch the developing scene.
Military police move in to restrain Frost, but they stand down*

at the wave of the Major General's hand.

FROST

"You son of a bitch! My friend gave her life so that we could get to this place in time to warn your pathetic ass and you couldn't even let us know. She didn't have to die!"

Oz rises to his feet. He wipes a small amount of blood from his now busted upper lip with the back of his hand.

OZ

"The fact that your friend thought it was necessary to risk her life so that you can get here is none of my concern."

Frost get's ready to electrify the disrespectful general, but is held back by Shay. The look in Shay's eyes tells Frost that he's not worth the energy.

OZ

"My responsibility is for the people in this base and making sure they are safe. Besides, Captain Taylor is in the infirmary recovering from her battle."

Oz points down the hall to the big red-cross that marks the infirmary. The two ladies run down the hallway, barge in and see a bandaged Rayne sleeping on a bed.

INT. MILITARY BASE-INFIRMARY

The girls walk up to her with tears rolling down their cheeks.
They smile to see their friend alive. Oz steps up to the doorway
and looks in on the ladies. He pauses for minute contemplating
if he should interrupt or let them have their reunion. He
chooses the former and walks into the room.

OZ

"Our scouts watched the whole battle unfold. Rayne
managed to take out most of demons headed this way.
She gave them hell right until the end. When the coast
was clear our scouts moved in, dug her out of the rubble,
and brought her here as fast as he could. You're
welcome."

Shay jumps up causing the Major General to flinch and take a
guarded stance, but is taken by surprise when she embraces
him in a fierce hug. Looking up at the Major General with a
slight sheen in her eyes, Shay smiles.

SHAY

"I was beginning to think that you were a complete
asshole, but you've proved me wrong."

Frost holds Rayne's hand as she stands up to address Oz. The
commotion in the room stirs Rayne and her eyes flutter open.

FROST

"Thank you for helping her."

Noticing that Rayne is awake, Shay turns to her excitedly.

SHAY

"Rayne you're alive!"

Frost turns around to see Rayne smiling at her. She leans down and hugs the battered woman.

FROST

"You crazy bitch."

Rayne is overjoyed and surprised when she receives a full on kiss on the lips from Frost.

RAYNE

"Good to see you too, Frosty."

Frost smiles at Rayne. Shay leans over Frost and hugs her injured Friend.

SHAY

"How are you doing, are you alright?"

RAYNE

"Oh my aging ass will be fine. I just need some R & R."

OZ

"Rest when you're dead soldier. Focus on healing up now. Everyone let the old war hero sleep."

Nurses begin to enter the room and check the monitors.

Another nurse prepares a needle to draw some blood for further testing, but one look from Rayne made her stop and put away the damned thing.

FROST

"You have to tell me everything when you get up. Rest easy chick."

Rayne waves at the ladies as they leave, winces at the sharp pain in her chest and then eases her arm down.

INT. MILITARY BASE-BARRACKS

Oz personally shows Frost and Shay where they can sleep. He takes them to a barracks where the other clansmen are resting for the night. Everyone looks uneasy and tired.

OZ

"You ladies can sleep here for the night. I suggest you get your rest. It's going to be a bloody day when those things get here."

FROST

"Well, that should help us rest easy tonight."

The ladies find empty bunks and settle in for the night. A single tear escapes Frost's eye. She quickly wipes the stray liquid emotion away and rests her head on the soft pillow. Frost doesn't notice how quickly she fades into a deep sleep.

CHAPTER 13

The next morning, Frost wakes up to the gentle tapping of little fingers. Her eyes open to see a little girl standing next to her bed. Her golden brown eyes are wide with wonder as she beams at Frost. Her lightly freckled face gleams with a sense of awe as she stares wide eyed at her. The complete sense of optimism in such bleak times baffles Frost.

EMALINE

"Hi!"

Frost sits up in her bunk then rubs her eyes of the night's dreamless sleep and looks at the golden eyed girl confused. She had never seen the youngster before and yet, there is a sense of familiarity when she meets her eyes. A skeptical expression creeps on to Frost's face.

FROST

"Hello."

The little girl squeals in delight at the greeting. Completely caught off guard by the little girls dancing in place, Frost doesn't really know how to respond to the child.

FROST

"Is there something you need? Help? Medication perhaps?"

Unfazed by Frost's sarcastic line of questioning the little girl continues to dance for a moment longer before answering in a thick Scottish brogue.

EMALINE

"I don't need help, but I am here to help you Frost Weaver. My grandfather and I have been looking for you for a very long time. I thought you'd be bigger."

At that moment an older gentleman walks into the barracks and dips his head in greeting. The little girl looks back to wave the man over, then she turns back to a very confused Frost with a huge gap toothed smile. Frost rubs the grogginess from her eyes.

The bearded man pulls a metal chair up to the bunk and sits. The little girl climbs onto his lap and swings her legs.

LAILOKEN

"Please excuse my granddaughter. She's just extremely happy to have found you."

Frost looks at the pair confused. She notices right away that they don't look like the others living in this cursed world. They're too clean and the hope has yet to leave their eyes. She doesn't know what's going on but she's sure that they are about to tell her. The question is, should she care.

LAILOKEN

"There really is no easy way to put this and telling you will only serve to make you doubt our journey. With that being said I would appreciate it if you let me show you."

More confused than ever, Frost just nods her head slowly. She wonders how he will show her. None of the tribes had access to technology. Only the military had those kinds of toys. Before her mind could go any farther, the man leans closer, moves his hand close to hers, and then stops.

LAILOKEN

"May I?"

Bewildered, Frost shies away. The little girl, Emaline smiles softly then nods toward her grandfather's waiting hand.

FROST

"May you what?"

Just then the wave of magical talent emanating from the pair crashes through Frost catching her completely by surprise.

LAILOKEN

"May I show you?"

Frost nods slowly. The bearded man takes her hand. Nothing happens and just as Frost was about to take back her hand, a tidal wave of energy washes over her. Images from an ancient past flicker through her mind like a slide show flavored with emotions. Images of an ancient war with the various creatures roaming the surface of the world fly through her mind. Then the images of the imprisonment of their leader zooms past almost so fast that she barely has time to register it. Then she can see the images of a strange man wearing clothing from her time being carried into this home. She then sees love blossom.

Lailoken struggles with the effort it takes to project the information he feels Frost needs. Emaline places her hand on his and lends him strength.

Frost's mouth gapes open. Her eyes roll back into her head as the sweat pours from her head down to her body. She can see the man from the future fighting with the King of the Demons. Then in a flash the man is gone. The next series of images are of the old man and his granddaughter walking through time searching. He then shows her the many ways the man of the futures dies and how her world dies with him. Tears stream down her face and then she passes out. When she awakes the old man and his granddaughter are gone.

CHAPTER 14

EXT. WASTELAND-OUTSKIRTS

A few days later, Izeta and what's left of his army reach the base. He scans the old base for activity. The reduced Legion looks on in anticipation of the battle that is to come. A grunt demon begins to jump up and down waving his arms frantically to get the attention of Izeta. Without looking at the demon he acknowledges him.

IZETA

"What is it?"

GRUNT DEMON

"Sir, it looks as if Solomn has found us."

The general looks over in the direction that the grunt has pointed and spots Solomn facing them on a hill side. The silhouette of the lone Prince stands out as the sun begins to rise behind him, encasing the young man in a beautiful halo.

IZETA

"That fool boy."

EXT. MILITARY BASE-WATCH TOWER

Returning from his trip to get coffee, or what passes for coffee, a soldier walks over to the window and spots Solomn off in the distance. He can barely make out who or what he is seeing because of the glare from the sun. He just appears as a lanky black mass. Turning to the other soldier that just seems to be stuck in a daze, Hucks shakes him and causes his head to sway in the opposite direction.

HUCKS

"Hey. Do you see that?"

GOMEZ

"Do you see that? There is a whole lot of shit on the opposite hill just waiting to cause a whole lotta hurt."

HUCKS

"What the hell is that?"

GOMEZ

"Holy mother of God."

Hucks dashes across the room and sounds the alarm. The high pitch screech of the sirens blare throughout the base waking those who sleep and telling who those who couldn't, that hell is at their door step.

Some soldiers run to mini gun turrets and others run to the weapons cache. The rest lead the woman and children to the blast bunker then seal the door. The pilots of the mech suits power up and go through their check lists.

MILITARY BASE-BARRACKS

Frost and Shay jump out of bed. They rush out to the hall to see what is going on. They look down the hallway and see Rayne limping their way strapping some new body armor to her chest.

RAYNE

"Come on ladies this ain't no drill!"

EXT. WASTELAND-OUTSKIRTS

Izeta hears the alarm sound and sends the remainder of his army charging towards the base. The beasts and monsters alike scream a soul clenching battle cry as they advance. Solomn watches the horde as the humans in the towers open fire. The mini guns drop thousands of shells as the rounds are being pumped out at lightning speed. Some demons make it to the gate and the moment they touch it they are electrified. Some immediately back away while others leap over the fifteen foot high barrier.

IZETA

"Those idiots!"

IZETA CONT'D

The general dismounts the Cerberus and turns to one of his soldiers. He points to Solomn.

"Watch the Prince. The second he moves I want you and your men on him but he is not to be harmed. Get me?"

Izeta walks on to the battlefield. Bullets whiz by his head and body. He calmly walks until he is a few yards in front of the main gate. He stops and begins to charge his energy. Izeta extends one hand and blows the gates apart.

The soldiers in the gun towers see that the small demon has taken out their first line of defense and focus all their fire on him. The battle hardened general gracefully dodges the bullets as they come inches from his body. He fires off another energy blast at one of the turrets destroying it and the men inside instantly. He calls for his army to move in. The fragmented Legion advances like a monstrous tsunami.

INT. MILITARY BASE-LAUNCH TERMINALS

Major General Oz rushes into the tiny control room and provides the two soldiers working there with the launch codes for the Black Matter warhead.

OZ

"You will launch on my order."

BAYBERRY

"Yes sir."

EXT. MILITARY BASE-MAIN GATES

A wall of heavily armed soldiers cut down the demons as they try to enter the base.

Rayne, Frost and Shay run to the frontlines. Frost was worried at first about how battle ready Rayne would be, but after seeing her move, all pretense of having to watch out for her are abandoned. It's like she was watching a professional dancer on stage.

RAYNE

"Save some for me boys!"

Rayne throws a grenade into the heart of the demon masses. The sphere explodes and Rayne is just thrilled to watch the spray of blood along with the body parts that fly in every direction.

Frost and Shay look at each other. They exchange a nod and jump into the fight. Other magic users join Frost and Shay in the massive battle. Each elemental warrior is worth at least ten men and they all know it. Many of them use the pain of watching their loved ones parish as motivation to kill as many beasts as they can. The thought of knowing what is at stake gives them the fuel to light their fires.

Shay creates a massive azure fireball and throws it into a squad of demons headed in her direction. The ball explodes on impact engulfing the band in a brilliant indigo fire.

Frost sprints toward Izeta cutting down every demon in her path while she imbues her sword with electric energy. Another magic user lunges at the demon general. The man tries to fight him, throwing a couple of charged strikes that are easily blocked and with a swipe of Izeta's sword the man is sliced in two.

Frost fires a lightning bolt that is dodged by the other worldly swordsman. He fires off a blast of his own that Frost dives over and lands in a roll, allowing the destructive force to fly right past her. The stray blast collides with a group humans and monstrous combatants blowing them apart. With only a meter between her and her target, Frost strikes with her sword. Izeta parries the blade with his own.

IZETA

"That's it girl. Show me what you've got!"

EXT. WASTELAND

Solomn's attention is wrenched away from the battle taking place below by the sound of stampeding soldiers. He follows the sound to find his father, Belial charging with a score of warriors ready to kill and not take prisoners. Solomn smiles inwardly. He doesn't care about the speed at which his father has made it to this place, he's just happy that he'll have his chance to end the man's existence.

INT. MILITARY BASE-WATCH TOWER

The soldiers in the watch tower relay the situation to their commanding officer and it is quickly reported to the Major General.

MECH SOLDIER

"Sir! We've got a shitload of hostiles heading our way! What are your orders?"

COMMANDER

"Stand firm Marine. We are sending assistance. It's going to be danger close so brace yourself."

EXT.MILITARY BASE-HANGERS

Giant steel doors open and fighter planes blast out of the hangers. Soldiers in mech suits make their way out the bay doors ready to even the odds.

The planes fly over to the battle and begin to fire their guns at the incoming enemy below. Another fighter plane fires hellfire missiles into the Legions, thinning their numbers drastically while the ground battle rages on. The mech suits are slow, but their .50 cal guns and crushing strength more than make up for it. They are quickly swarmed by humans who have been infected with the manticore. The terrible things begin pulling on the limbs of the giant robotic suits trying to get at the men and women inside.

EXT. MILITARY BASE-FRONTLINES

Frost and Izeta battle it out on the packed battle field. Monsters and humans die around them. Their swords clash with great speed and skill. With the sun rising in the sky, the orange yellow light flickers off their balanced weapons as they blur with every clash. Izeta finds an opening and takes it. He stops his sword inches from Frost's throat, smiles then returns to a ready stance. Frost leaps backward. He had her and he didn't follow through. She pushes the implications aside and continues the fight.

Shay catches a glimpse of her friend and the high demon fighting. She can't help but think that they look like two samurai dueling as the tracer bullets, missiles and bodies rain down around them. Shay and Rayne team up on the battlefield. The two incinerate demons in their path. Shay runs up then jumps off the back of a colossal demon then fires a massive fire ball in its face once she passes over it. The demon begins to swing its weapon wildly smashing humans and demons alike. Rayne runs up to the demon and jumps on its back, clinging to its neck as if she were a small monkey. She slaps a sticky C10 grenade to its face and jumps off right before it explodes. The brilliant explosion blows apart the monster leaving only a crater in its wake.

CHAPTER 15

EXT. MILITARY BASE- BATTLEFIELD

Belial knows that the planes are a big factor of this battle so he starts to fire massive energy waves at them, taking out the engines of a few and completely destroying others.

The pilots going down try to steer their damaged aircraft into large masses of demons right before they eject. The canopies pop and the pilots use their jet packs to slow their descent. Some don't make it out in time. The pilots that were able to eject, pull out their machine pistols and begin to fire as they drift back to solid ground.

Belial spots the men and women who have left their doomed aircrafts and though they don't pose an immediate threat, he jumps to kill them as they draw closer to landing in the chaotic mess. Out of ten mech suits, only four are left standing, carrying on the fight. Their battered frames leak cooling fluid and begin to overheat.

Solomn runs toward the battlefield to assist the humans. He jumps into the heart of the battle, grabbing a demon from the back and ripping its throat out before moving on to the next.

He delivers a series of machine gun punches to its chest then upper cuts it and blasts the demon in mid air. He turns around and stops his attack when he sees that Shay is at his back. They have a split second standoff. Solomn quickly moves Shay out of the way of a blast that would have surely blown her apart. The rebellious Prince looks at the bewildered woman and nods his head. She nods back and they continue to fight side by side. Shay didn't have time to think about the unlikely alliance, but she was glad it was there.

Belial takes out a good number of planes before they have been called back due to lack of resources and extensive damage. Belial turns his attention to where the main battle is taking place and realizes that his son, Solomn is helping the humans. Belial becomes enraged and charges at his son.

Frost and Izeta continue to battle amidst all the chaos. The older swordsman counters Frost's strike and fires an energy ball into her center mass. She manages to catch the orb in her hand, using her electrical energy as buffer to keep it from blowing her hand apart. Still holding the small but dense energy ball, she raises her arm and sends it flying into a mob of demons behind her. Izeta looks on impressed and even gives Frost a round of golf claps.

IZETA

"Impressive, your family must truly be the descendents of the spiritual warrior, Michael. It's a shame someone as talented as you must die here."

Frost throws her sword and runs at Izeta delivering a barrage of charged strikes landing each one in pressure points disabling the demon. Catching the swordsman off guard and stunning him. Frost looks at the dazed general, wondering why he is smiling. She pushes the question out of her mind. She catches her sword and thrusts it up to the hilt into his neck. She delivers a focused charge of explosive lightning that runs through the sword and into his flesh, causing his head to explode. Frost is left dazed from her last attack. The body of Izeta falls to the ground. The battle continues as she watches so many people and demons dying all around her. Some she knew, most she didn't know at all. They all would die in the end.

Shay looks over at Frost and realizes that an enraged Belial is headed straight for her dazed friend. Belial charges at Frost with the bloody tip of his spear pointed directly at her spine. At the last second, Shay pushes Frost out of the way as the spear is rammed straight through her body. Shay coughs up blood as she grabs the shaft. Teeth gritted, Shay tries to pull the metal shaft out of her body.

RAYNE

"Shay!"

Rayne kills the beast she was fighting and runs toward her impaled friend. Belial lifts his spear with Shay still at its tip. Shay screams in agony as she is being lifted off the ground. She holds onto the shaft with one hand to keep from slipping forward on the weapon. With her last ounce of energy, Shay lifts her hand and charges a fire ball. Just as she discharges the ball of fire, the Demon King flicks his body, causing her shot to go wild. Shay's limp body flies off the tip of the spear and into

Rayne.

The soldiers focus their fire at the rest of the dwindling demons. Solomn runs toward Belial who is getting ready to ram his spear into his slow to recover half sister.

SOLOMN

"I'm not going to make it."

Solomn lets loose an energy blast at his father. Belial knows the attack is coming and deflects it at the cost of his spear that shatters in his grasp. Frost snaps out of her daze to realize what is going on and moves out of Belial's attack range, with quick and measured leaps backward. Belial tosses the shattered spear to the ground.

BELIAL

"You dare attack me! Your own father? You sack of wasted flesh of blood!"

SOLOMN

"You killed my mother and now it's time we end this, father."

Solomn charges at his father and strikes with a right hook. Belial counters with his own right hand and their fist collide, causing a shockwave to rip through the air. Rayne holds Shay, watching her as she takes her last gasps of air as the blood fills her lungs. Shay stops breathing. Her shimmering emerald eyes are wide open as a single tear slowly rolls down the side of her face. Rayne wipes the blood away from Shays face and cleans the blood around her mouth. She runs her hand over the jade eyes of Shay so that they close.

The remaining gun turrets blast at the last remaining demons. While the soldiers and spell casters desperately fight for their lives to finish off the few demons left on the battlefield.

Frost runs over to where Rayne holds Shay. Frost collapses to the ground. She cries for her fallen friend. Frost grabs her Shay, pulls her up, and holds her close. Frost looks over at Belial as he fights a slender demon and her hate boils over, causing her to shake violently.

Belial catches his son's kick then punches him in the face and throws him near Frost. Solomn hits the ground sliding, before he flips and tumbles out to regain control.

BELIAL

"Your mother was a useless whore who over played her hand. Her very existence annoyed me. It was only fitting that she'd die at the hands of her equally pathetic daughter."

Frost lays Shay down and rises to her feet. Ignoring the fact that the half man fighting alongside her is her brother, she moves forward with vengeful purpose.

FROST

"You fucking bastard!"

Frost slashes at Belial but he easily dodges her attacks. She was only able to slice a bit of his armor, taking out a chunk of metal.

Solomn runs at his father right side behind Frost. Belial swings his fist and backhands Frost, knocking her off to the side then he grabs Belial's hand, swings him around so they are back to back. The Prince then reaches over his shoulder grabbing Belial's head, wrenching him over and knee lifts his father in the face, knocking him on his ass.

Solomn runs at Belial and kicks him in the face, sending him grinding through the dirt to crash into a massive boulder. The half human Prince follows up his attack with a powerful energy blast that hits Belial and explodes. The dust settles from the explosion. The rock is completely obliterated, but Belial is nowhere to be found. The Prince searches for his father, then Belial materializes behind his son and punches him so hard that the armor that shielded his back shatters. Frost stumbles to her feet and watches in horror as Belial's arm is completely through Solomn's chest. The half human man looks down at his father's bloody fist that seems to be growing from his chest in shock. He goes to grab his father's hand, but it is ripped back through the way it came. Solomn falls to his knees as Belial walks around to face him.

Belial takes hold of his son's head and removes his mask. He then lifts the dying Prince back to his feet and holds him upright.

BELIAL

"Did you really think you could take me out boy?"

Solomn begins to cough up blood. The half man struggles to keep his eyes open.

BELIAL CONT'D

"My first mistake was thinking I could have an heir that was worthy of my blood with a human. You disgust me."

Belial throws his beaten son to the hard ground and begins to kick the fallen man. Rayne jumps on Belial's back, slamming her plasma daggers into his chest. In a instant, she too is thrown to the ground with such force that the air escapes her lungs leaving her gasping and coughing. The Demon King lifts his leg to stomp on the gasping woman, but she rolls out of the way and on to her feet. Calmly walking toward Rayne, Belial can't help but snort and spit on the ground before her.

BELIAL

"I'm going to tear you limb from limb, bitch."

Rayne ignites her plasma daggers. She smiles at the large man and invites him forward.

RAYNE

"I'll be your huckleberry."

Rayne smiles deviously as she turns off one of her plasma blades and pulls out her detonator. Belial stops, looks at the device, then begins to reach for his back but the armor restricts his movements. Just as Rayne positions her thumb above the switch, Belial teleports to her and grabs her instantly. They struggle for control.

"You can't stop it mother fucker. You're gonna burn."

Rayne spits in his eyes, then uses her chin to push the little red button, setting off the C10 she placed on Belial's back when she jumped on him. Rayne is blown away from Belial, smashes through a small perimeter fence and into the wall of the compound. The smoke begins to clear to reveal Belial, standing in the crater left by the blast. His armor is completely destroyed. Various parts of his body are burnt and bleeding. Belial looks at the injured female soldier with pure loathing.

Rayne sits up then falls back down. She looks down and pulls a piece of the fence out of her side. She looks up to see Belial with his mechanical arm extended, charging up a blast that will surely kill her.

Solomn Jumps on Belial's legs, sending the tiny ball straight into the air as they fall to the ground. Frost runs to Rayne and helps her up.

RAYNE

"If you've got some special trick up your sleeve you better use it now. That guy's a beast."

Frost hands Rayne off to the soldiers that are heading back into the base with wounded.

FROST

Looking Rayne in the eye:

"I have one more thing to try, but I need some time."

SGT. CONWAY

"You heard her Marines! Let's buy the lady some time."

Two soldiers carry Rayne into the base, while the others move into position to begin their assault.

CHAPTER 16

INT. MILITARY BASE-LAUNCH ROOM

The small command room is dim. The blinking ready lights from the once state of the art computers, share their light with the men working by them. Oz watches the monitors and is well aware of what is taking place outside. Most of the exterior cameras have been destroyed, but a few are left to capture and record the scene.

OZ

"Here are your coordinates. Let's hope this weapon still works."

The two men punch in the coordinates and get ready to launch the warheads at every major demon held stronghold across the globe.

EXT. MILITARY BASE-BATTLEFIELD

The battle grounds are littered with the corpses of humans and beasts alike. Blood and ichor saturate the dirt.

Frost sneaks into Belial's blind spot then raises her arms and begins to focus all of her energy into a single point just as the old man instructed her. Belial doesn't notice the soldiers that are ready to fire on him. Solomn knows that this is his last chance to avenge his mother. He focuses his last ounce of willpower to lift his broken body off of the cold ground, leaps onto his father's back and holds on tight as Belial pulls himself up off the ground. Solomn can see the soldiers aiming their big guns, so he plants his feet firmly in the dirt and uses his body as an anchor to hold his father in place.

SOLOMN

"What are you waiting for?! Do it now!"

The soldiers open fire on the two demons. The bullets pass through both of them. Blood and chunks of bones are sprayed everywhere.

Sololmn falls to the ground dead, while Belial takes the spray of bullets head on. Step by step Belial falls back. Bullets ricochet off his metal arm while others pass straight through his body.

The soldiers empty their magazines, step back to reload while the second wave prepares to fire. Belial uses this time to fire off a blast killing one soldier. He teleports to another, wrenching the man's head to one side, snapping his neck, and then he begins to kill them one by one.

Frost continues to focus her energy into a single point. A tiny black dot opens, ripping the fabric of space, and swirling as it grows. The winds generated by this act are tremendous. She finds it hard to stay on her feet and not be blown back. The *black-hole continues to grow. Oddly enough, stones begin to fly out of it as it generates its power.*

INT. MILITARY BASE-LAUNCH ROOM

Oz looks at his men controlling the computers and walks over to the monitors that are recording the battle outside.

OZ

"Launch the warheads at the stains those monsters call home now."

The men punch in the launch codes and slide in their keys. They count down from three then turn them.

EXT. MILITARY MISSILE SILO

The doors to the missile bays open and the warheads come screaming out of the hidden chambers. The smoky fire fills the air with a thunderous boom and the smell of burnt ozone.

EXT. MILITARY BASE-BATTLE GROUNDS

The missiles can be seen flying over head. The warheads produce a roaring thunder as they streak overhead.

Belial looks up at the warheads passing above him, still clutching a dying Marine in his hands and then the winds from the wormhole snatch his attention. His eyes grow wide with recognition. He has seen this before. In utter shock, Belial stands frozen.

BELIAL

"No. It can't be."

Belial drops the bleeding soldier. Just as he starts to make his way toward Frost, a grenade bounces on the ground, rolls, and explodes right in front of him, knocking him on his back. Rayne smiles as she leans against the large door frame leading into the base and then falls to the floor unconscious. Belial slowly picks himself up. He doesn't take his eyes off of the wormhole for a second.

CHAPTER 17

EXT. MILITARY BASE-BATTLE GROUNDS

Frost screams as she tries to maintain the vast amount of power needed to keep the gateway open. Right before her talent is completely drained, a man in tattered clothes flies out of the hole and crumbles to the ground. The sky crackles and lightning streaks down from the sky. The man begins to stagger to his feet, when a flash of light fills the sky from the explosion way off in the distance. The tip very of a mushroom cloud can be seen rising into the air and fading into the atmosphere.

The man looks around, amazed at all the carnage around him and then he spots Belial.

BELIAL

"You."

MICHAEL

"Me."

Michael turns on his A.X.L. He charges at Belial and swipes at him with his laser cutter. Belial side steps his attack and uses his mechanical arm to strike Michael with an elbow to the face. Michael jumps back and rubs his face.

MICHAEL

"I see you got a new arm. You know I'm gonna take it."

Michael slashes with his laser sword, but only manages to slice his foes chest. Belial jumps back and fires off an energy blast. At that same moment, Michael puts his hands out to use his energy as a shield, but the force is too strong. Belial's powerful blast shatters Michael's shield like glass and blows him back. Michael hits the ground and turns off his sword as he rises to his feet only to find that Belial is right in front of him, in the middle of an attack he cannot counter. Belial smashes Michael in the face, flinging him into the air. Before Michael can fly too high, Belial grabs Michael's ankle and slams him back into the ground. Frost runs behind Belial. Once she is close enough, she rams her sword into the Demon Kings side and begins to twist.

Belial stops for a moment, only to look down in search of the source of the pain and finds the sword buried to the hilt in his body. Belial whips around and grabs Frost by the neck. He begins to hammer her in the gut and face. Belial looks at the nearly unconscious girl and flings her away from him. Almost lifeless, Frost soars through the air like a ragdoll before she slam into the hard ground.

Belial rips the sword from his body, tosses it away, and focuses his attention back to Michael who is still trying to get up. Michael struggles to climb to his feet. Once he is able to stand he finds that can barely lift his arms, let alone defend himself.

MICHAEL

"Is that all you've got?"

Enraged, Belial marches toward the helpless man and takes hold of his hair pulling his head back. Belial begins punching the wounded man in the face. The King of Demons screams in frustration with every strike.

BELIAL

"Why won't you die?"

Michael's arms fall limply to his side during the attack while his legs begin to buckle. Belial releases his hold on Michael and lets him fall to the ground. The remaining soldiers and magic casters retreat back to the base while a handful remain to finish off the stragglers. The few spell casters charge in while the last of the mechs still standing offer support with their massive guns and fire on Belial. The demon turns his attention to the men and woman coming his way. The King of Monsters runs to the nearest caster, grabs him, and uses him as a shield to guard himself from the storm of bullets. Then he continues to run toward the Marines with lightning speed. Belial throws the corpse toward the soldiers and begins to tear them apart. He takes a gun from one soldier and impales a female caster who was charging in for an attack. The rage filled demon begins to pounce on the mechs and tear away their armor.

EXT. MILITARY BASE-BATTLE GROUNDS

Frost begins to regain consciousness and tries to pick herself up, but can't find the strength. She looks up to see that Michael is laying motionless face down on the ground. She also notices Belial fighting off Marines and other casters. She saw this very moment in a vision the old man had shown her.

Frost begins to drag herself across the battlefield, inching her way toward Michael. Every movement sends waves of pain through her body and tears begin to roll down her face. The sounds of people dying around her fades as she focuses on getting to Michael. Frost grits her teeth and picks herself up off the ground. She begins to stumble toward the man she seemingly pulled out of thin air. With each step the pain gets more intense. Finally she falls at Michael's side, places her hand at the middle of his back. She begins to heal and transfer what little energy she can spare to Michael reviving him.

Michael awakes to see Frost struggling to finish the spell. Frost looks at Michael then passes out. Michael stands up to see Belial fighting the remaining mages. Michael raises his arm and begins to fire his gun. Each shot is driven into the thick of Belial's back. In a rage, the Demon King lets out a tremendous roar and a shock wave erupts from his body that throws his opponents away from him. Michael runs at Belial still shooting, landing every shot.

Belial turns to face Michael then disappears. Michael stops dead in his tracks. On the defensive, Michael looks in every direction to see where the demon might appear. Belial appears and Michael fires off a shot only to see that Belial disappeared before the round could hit him. Michael stays on guard, his eyes wide open waiting for his chance to strike. Belial appears then disappears again and again, toying with Michael.

MICHAEL

"Come on out! Let's finish this!"

Belial appears behind Michael and punches him in the back shattering his armor. The blow knocks him forward. Michael turns around and finds that Belial is not there. Michael hears a high pitched sound come from behind him, turns around using his energy as a shield again to block the blast. Belial appears behind Michael and kicks him in the back sending him flying. When Michael hits the ground, he rolls and he uses that momentum to jump back on his feet. Again, the King of Demons is nowhere to be found, leaving Michael to search for him. Finding nothing but dirt, rocks, and shattered corpses Michael waits. Another high pitched sound catches Michael's attention, but this time he uses his energy to shoot himself into the air. While airborne, Michael can see the energy ball explode on impact with the ground, throwing chunks of earth in every direction and leaving behind a small crater. Michael catches some flickering movement off to his side and knows that it's Belial moving in for the attack. Michael pushes his energy down again lifting himself higher into the air. With a twist along with a bit of luck, Michael kicks and feels the resistance of flesh. He knows that he caught the bastard. Michael's swift kick lands squarely on the side of the head, just as Belial appears, knocking the demon back to the ground in a heap.

Michael fires a few more rounds from his gun at Belial before landing on the ground hard. He pulls out his sword again and turns it on. Belial shoots out of the crater and lands in a fierce ready stance to face Michael.

The two combatants charge toward each other. Michael strikes with his blade and Belial with his cybernetic arm. They both catch the others attack and struggle for control over the other. To on lookers it would seem that all martial training had just been thrown out to the wind as the man and demon battle for the upper hand. Belial uses his head as a weapon and slams it into Michael's nose smashing it and causing him to drop his sword. Belial uses that little bit of time to take hold of Michael's throat in a crushing grip. Then he leaps into the air putting several meters between them and the earth. Once airborne, Belial throws Michael back down to smash into a huge boulder and roll off. Still hovering in the air, the powerful King raises his hand to charge a massive energy ball.

BELIAL

"I've waited 1600 years for this! It's finally over!"

With his body aching from all the punishment he has taken, Michael struggles to pick himself up. With some effort he raises his head, smiling with grim determination and looks up at Belial just as the Demon King thrust the massive ball of destruction down towards him. Michael uses what he has learned from Lailoken and tries to push the ball back at Belial. The strain of trying to push the giant ball of shimmering energy is almost too much for Michael to bear. The two men are locked in a power battle, each trying to overpower the other. Demon and man push the ball of death toward each other.

Michael feels his strength flagging. The massive ball begins inching its way toward Michael. Belial begins to laugh as Michael drops down to one knee, unable to withstand the force that is pushing him down. The demon laughs because he knows his victory is only a few short moments away.

CHAPTER 18

EXT. MILITARY BASE-BATTLE GROUNDS

Frost regains consciousness and a little of her strength, then pulls out her spiked whip chains ready to rejoin the fight. Belial is so focused on Michael that he does not notice the fierce woman moving into the ideal flanking position.

Frost cocks back her hand and hurls the tethered spikes at Belial. The chained spikes penetrate his back, causing the unrelenting demon to lose his concentration. With Belial distracted, Michael is able to gain a few more feet as he regains his footing and pushes the ball toward his enemy.

FROST

"Nineteen years of suffering! Nineteen years of pain!"

Screaming from the exertion of energy, Frost lets loose a massive surge of electrical energy. The current flies through the chains and into the spikes embedded in Belial's back.

The Demon King is powerless to stop the amount of electric energy flowing through him. This turn of events allows

---

Michael to gain the upper hand and push the ball of explosive energy into him where it erupts in a brilliant flash of devastating force. Belial plummets to the ground still being electrocuted by Frost.

Frost stops the current and falls to her knees exhausted. Michael picks up his laser cutter and walks up to the fallen demon. Michael stomps on Belial's chest pinning him down.

MICHAEL

"I told you that I would take your head."

Still trembling and skin scorched from the shock, Belial looks up at Michael. His eyes reflect the fear that grows in his heart. A large crow lands on one of the destroyed towers and caws.

BELIAL

"Killing me changes nothing."

MICHAEL

"Maybe not, but it is one hell of a start."

Michael swings his blade and sends Belial's head rolling across the bloody battlefield. Frost sits on the ground fighting to stay awake. The soldiers inside the base slowly make their way out. Michael looks at the T.D.B and punches in the date and time before he had been sucked through the wormhole. The band displays an error message. Frustrated, Michael runs over to Frost and picks her up off the ground.

MICHAEL

"How did you bring me here? I need you to send me
back."

*Frost tries to stay awake but her body refuses to listen to the
signals sent from her brain.*

MICHAEL CONT'D

"Wake up! I need you to send me back to where I was!
Wake up!"

FROST

"I… I don't have the energy."

*The other people emerging from inside the base watch in
confusion. Then a little girl, no older than ten walks out from
the crowd of people and up to Michael to stand beside him.*

EMALINE

"You don't need her to go where you want to go. Nor do
you need this device."

*Michael looks at the girl, confusion written across his face. He
kneels down to her eye level.*

MICHAEL

"You know how to send me back?"

EMALINE

Shaking her head:

"No. I don't know how to do it, but my grandfather once told me how one is supposed to do it."

MICHAEL

"Your grandfather? Who? How?"

Leaning close to Michael as if it were a secret, she bops him on the head and smiles.

EMALINE

"It's all in the mind. Focus on a single point and what you need. It will happen."

Michael knows that after what he has just been through he does not have the energy to attempt such a thing. He hangs his head in defeat and then the little girl places her hand on his. Michael looks at her and sees that she is smiling. Then he feels an immense surge of energy flow through her hand and into him. She smiles warmly at him.

EMALINE

"You should take a few steps back now."

Michael steps back and closes his eyes. Thoughts of the last time he saw Una fills his mind, then he opens his eyes and looks at a single point on a rock to focus on. For a few moments nothing happens. He glances back at the little girl and she nods her head as if to say, "Keep going." Michael turns his attention back to the small rock.

Officers begin to make their way toward Michael shouting orders, but he completely ignores them and focuses harder. The wind starts to pick up causing the soldiers and onlookers to take cautious steps back. The rock begins to distort and open up slowly. The tiny hole appears. It begins to pull debris into it as it grows wider and stronger. Once the gate is wide enough, Michael looks back at Emaline. The tiny girl winks and smiles at Michael before he jumps into the wormhole. The hole closes and the people look at the little girl in amazement. The soldiers snap out of their shock and move out to collect the wounded. Fresh soldiers move out to finish off any creatures still left alive. A med team heads out to Frost and begin treating her injuries before carrying her, along with the wounded into the base for medical attention.

INT. MILITARY BASE

OLD WOMAN

"Who was that, dear?"

EMALINE

"That was the father, Michael."

Emaline looks over to see her grandfather standing at the mouth of the bay doors. She runs to him and hugs him.

EMALINE

"He came just like you said he would."

LAILOKEN

"And you told him what to do."

EMALINE

"I did and it worked just like you said it would."

LAILOKEN

Smiling:

"Good. Now, let's go to the infirmary to see how your great granddaughter, Frost is doing."

The two walk down the hall together hand and hand then disappear into the crowd.

CHAPTER 19

EXT. GRASSY MOUNTAIN SIDE

The cold drizzle continues to fall from the sky but Una barely notices. She and her father stand at the edge of the cliff baffled by what they have just witnessed. Lailoken takes Una's hand then her bicep and helps her to her feet. Lailoken and Una hear a great thunder behind them. They both turn expecting the worst. Michael tumbles through the wormhole and hits the ground running. He runs past them and leaps off the mountain. Belial opens his eyes to see Michael hurdling through the air at him. Belial tries to move, but Michael uses an energy push to slam the crippled demon deeper into the ground.

EXT. MOUNTAIN-BASE

Michael whips out his laser cutter and rams it hard as he can into Belial's neck. The ancient thing shrieks in true terror as it's flesh and nerves are seared. Belial's body jerks violently.

MICHAEL

"You didn't think that you would get off that easy did you?"

Michael jerks the hot blade to the side severing Belial's head from his body and then blasts it into bloody chunks of organic confetti with his gun. The battered man looks up at Una and they both smile at each other. Michael switches off his blade and uses his energy push to leap from rock to rock until he makes his way up to his love.

EXT. GRASSY MOUNTAIN EDGE

Una runs up to Michael once he has landed on solid ground, hugs him, slaps him, and then kisses him deeply before resting her head on his shoulder crying.

UNA

"I was so worried."

LAILOKEN

Placing his hand on Michaels shoulder:

"You made it back."

Michael and Una look at each other. Michael wipes her tears away. They kiss deeply and passionately. Lailoken scratches his head, and rubs his foot in the mud. Finally after some time, he clears his throat. The two lovers rest their heads on one another and chuckle softly.

"This rain is pretty cold. We should head back home to warm up and tend to your wounds. "

Michael, along with Una and her father make their way back to the forest. The walk back to the homey cave was silent. The small family reflects on the morning's events and wonder if the dark shadow that plagued the world is finally gone or if they had only delayed its dark embrace over mankind.

INT. LAILOKEN'S CAVE

Once back in the relative safety and warmth of their dwelling, they shed their wet clothing for dry furs. Lailoken and Una prepare a healing beverage for the wounded warrior resting in the next chamber. Una grinds some dried herbs into a fine powder then pours them into the mixture her father has waiting on the table. Una looks up at her father when she notices the tension in his muscles.

UNA

"Father?"

Lailoken snaps out of his daze to look his daughter in the eyes. A gentle smile ruffles his beard and he pats her hands. They both turn to enter the room where Michael rests.

AUGURY

EPILOGUE

EXT. ROCKY BEACH

The waves crash along the shore of the beach. The storm that carried the soft cold drizzle of rain has moved on to other parts of the land. The dark viscous blood of the fallen King still blankets the hard jagged stones. What's left of his body lies motionless on the cold uneven ground. Unable to regenerate and no signals from the brain, the heart in his chest slows its beating.

A crow swoops down from the sky to land a top the severed head of Belial. It caws once before hopping off to land on the ground next to blood spattered head. The unnaturally large bird caws again while examining the lifeless eyes of the demon. Seeing no reaction from the gory head, the crow hops backward a few paces. The big black bird pecks out the dead elf's eyes and swallows them whole. A faint vermillion glow radiates from its dark beady eyes then its body contorts violently. Its legs grow thicker and larger. The dark feathers of its wings shrink into its skin, while the long dark beak retracts into its face. The process lasts for only half a second and when it is all done, a beautiful near naked woman stands before the head smiling.

Her long dark flowing hair falls over her perky breasts. Feathers stretch from her navel down to her thighs like a short skirt. Feathers run from her wrist to her elbows like a silky gauntlet.

She crouches down to take a handful of the dark elf's hair, then raises the head up to eye level, as she straightens her toned slender legs. Her full lipped smile softens, her angelic yet, predatory face. Her smile turns into a chuckle and from that hardy laughter escapes her throat.

MORRIGAN

"You fool child. You should have heeded my words.
Look at you now. What a waste. Too bad your older
brother has no desire to lead his people. You chose the
wrong path."

*The Goddess lets the head fall from her hands and with fluid
grace, she punts it into the sea. She watches the head bob in the
ocean waves before it fills with water and then sinks.*

*The pale woman shifts back to the large black bird. She caws as
if still laughing, then takes flight. Once high enough to clear
the mountain, Morrigan banks sharply and heads toward a
nearby grove so that she can return to Tír na nÓg and prepare
for what is to come. She has great plans for the bloodline of
Michael and Una, if they are willing to listen.*

E.A. Rodriguez

ABOUT THE AUTHOR

Enrique A. Rodriguez is an American writer with a love for science fiction, fantasy novels, movies and some anime. In his younger years he trained in many different forms of martial arts and often competed with his friends in friendly combative competitions. He also enjoys drawing and painting. He now resides in Kentucky with his wife and three daughters.